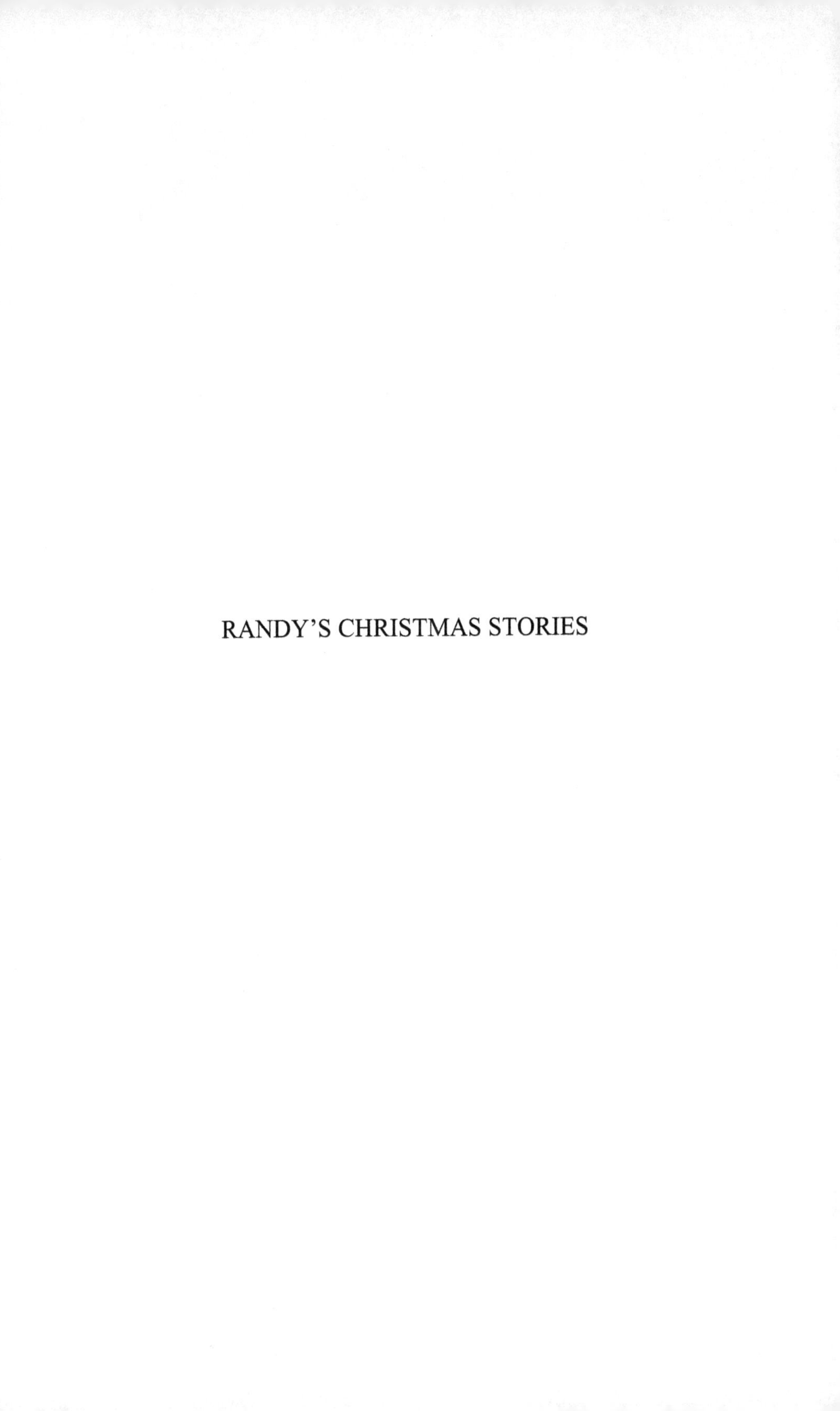

RANDY'S CHRISTMAS STORIES

RANDY'S CHRISTMAS STORIES

RANDY RAWLS

Rawls, Randy
Randy's Christmas Stories / Fun stories involving Christmas

Amazon Author Page
www.amazon.com/author/randyrawls

ISBN: 9798694163743

PREVIOUS WORKS FROM RANDY RAWLS

<u>Josh Hawkins</u>
Flight From Freedom
Justice Secured

<u>Beth Bowman</u>
Hot Rocks
Best Defense
Dating Death
Saving Dabba
Linda's Mom

<u>Standalones</u>
Jingle and His Magnificent Seven

<u>Tom Jeffries</u>
Thorns on Roses
The Runaway

<u>Historical</u>
Down by the River

<u>Ace Edwards</u>
Jake's Burn
Joseph's Kidnapping
Jade's Photos
Jingle's Christmas
Jasmine's Fate
Jeb's Deception

DEDICATION

For Tracy and David, my children, with my love.
For Joanne at *Murder on the Beach Mystery Bookstore*,
Delray Beach, FL, a friend to every author.
A special dedication to Jon Spisiak, a special friend who
recently left us.
To Sue Darst, a friend for many years, who inspired several
Of the stories.
And especially, for readers everywhere. Where would we be
without them?

ACKNOWLEDGMENTS

I absolutely must acknowledge the members of my critique group. They tolerate me, they help me, and they smile at the right times. Also, they cut me off at the knees when I need it. Thank you Ann, Gregg, RC, Stephanie, and Vicki. Special acknowledgment to. Also, a special acknowledgment to Sue Darst who gave a last read-through to my stories and blessed them.

Thank you, one and all.

WELCOME

This series of stories are written for anyone who enjoys Christmas or Christmas characters. I offer Jingle Bell, a Christmas elf, Joseph, a cattle-herding burro, and Ace Edwards, a Dallas PI.

First, we start by answering the question of how elves got to the North Pole to work for Santa. You'll find out in *Santa and the Leprechauns*.

From there, we enjoy Jingle Bell's adventures, discovering what an adventuresome and loyal elf he is.

Joseph takes the spotlight next. He is a wonderful burro who loves his herd, his owners, and those who share the Darst Ranch with him.

Then, we finish with Ace Edwards, Dallas PI. Ace's stories are a bit different, but still have Christmas as their central theme. Ace is not the normal hard-nosed PI who breaks heads first and then asks question. He has compassion and love for his fellow man.

Now that you know where we're headed, I can only hope you will enjoy my stories and look forward to more.

Of course, a review on Amazon.com is always appreciated.

AUTHOR COMMENT: Have you ever wondered how Santa makes all those toys? How elves somehow made it to the North Pole to help him? So have I. It was when this story came to me that I knew.

SANTA AND THE LEPRECHAUNS

Sean scurried from tree to tree, his crock of gold pressed against his chest. His breath was raspy because he'd been moving fast and hard for the past ten minutes. He spotted a large bush and scooted behind it, peeking through its branches along his backtrail to see if anyone followed. Seeing no one, he set the crock down with a grunt, then flattened himself beside it, staring under the bottom of the brambles. "I'll rest just a teeny bit," he said, closing his eyes. "So tired."

He jerked his head up from the ground. "Oh no, I fell asleep. My gold, where is my gold?" Rolling over, he wrapped his arms around the pot. "Thanks goodness, it's safe. No one found me."

With one hand on the crock, he took a large green handkerchief from his pocket and wiped his brow. "Can't be too careful. Too many people after my fortune. That big farmer got too close yesterday. He might still be after me. I have to find a safe place."

Sean was a leprechaun, a variety of elves found in Ireland. He was two-feet tall, making him one of the biggest in his village. His clothing was forest green—from his pointed sneakers to his pointed hat. Like all leprechauns, he possessed certain magic, a pot of gold, and a fear a human would catch him. If that occurred, tradition dictated that Sean reveal where he hid his treasure, in which case the human would have every right to it. There was also the danger someone, even another leprechaun, would discover his gold and steal it. However, unlike other of the wee people, he allowed his fear of losing his gold to make him bitter and untrusting of others. He spent most of his time away from his village, looking for the perfect hiding place and staring behind him, afraid there might be someone following.

After counting to fifty, he sneaked another peek under the bush. "Can't see anyone, but they might be hiding. I'd better move." He picked up the crock and dashed behind a large tree nearby, pressing himself into the bark. Another peek, another sigh as he settled to the ground. "Gotta find a place to bury this for tonight. Then I can go home for dinner."

Sean studied the base of the tree and its roots crawling along the top of the ground for yards in every direction. Studying the area, he saw the tree was the biggest around, at least five-hundred years old, he guessed.

He peeked around the forest again, then back at the roots. "I can hide my crock under that one where the water washed the dirt away. Once I fill it in, no one will find my gold. Maybe I can booby-trap it with sharp sticks." He grinned, enjoying the idea of punishing anyone who might try to steal his gold. Lifting the heavy crock, he moved to the spot.

When he sat the pot over the hole, it did not fit. "Bah," he said. "I'll have to enlarge it." Looking around, he spotted a broken branch and raced to grab it, his eyes never leaving his treasure. Digging as fast as he could, he made the pit big enough for his pot to fit inside, then pushed dirt over it. Finished, he ran to look behind each tree. After finding no one spying on him, he gathered sticks and brambles and banked them over the pot. A couple of times, he pricked himself on their points. Instead of saying ouch, he smiled. Anyone after his gold would pay a price.

He checked what he'd done, then began to dance a jig around the site. "They'll never find it here, they'll never find it here," he sang in his squeaky voice, followed by an elfin giggle, even as his beady eyes studied the forest.

His hat tumbled off, falling onto the fresh pile of dirt, sticking on one of the briars. He skipped around the hat, packing the ground where he'd buried the crock.

Splat. A large raindrop splashed against his forehead. He stopped dancing and looked up. Three more drops hit his face. "Oh no, rain," he cried, staring at the spot where his fortune lay buried.

A flash of lightning followed by the roar of thunder caused Sean to flinch. For a moment, his fear of the lightning was stronger than his love of his gold. "No more lightning," he whimpered. "I'm afraid of it."

But his call went unanswered. A September storm rolled in on the heels of the first crash. The wind blew and soon howled, sending twigs, branches, and other debris slashing through the air. Sean's hat spun upward where it snagged on a limb, flapping like a flag in a hurricane. Sean ran for the safety of the tree trunk, but an angry blast caught him and threw him to the ground. It rolled him over until his head slammed into an upraised root. Woozy, he grabbed on and wrapped his arms and legs around it. "Go away lightning. Go away thunder. Rain, please don't wash the dirt away from my gold. Someone will see it," he wailed. Branches tore free and crashing sounds resounded through the forest as trees tumbled. Sean hung on, worried, and sobbed for himself and his gold.

* * *

As Sean scrambled through the woods looking for the perfect hiding place, Santa rode high above in a practice run for his Christmas Eve adventure. It was still two months before letters from children would begin arriving so he used last year's list. It lay in his lap, and he ticked off each house as he flew over, verifying the names. He made notations where new babies had been born.

Occasionally, he frowned and put a mark beside the name of someone who had been naughty. When he returned to the North Pole, he'd estimate the number and type of toys needed—and the lumps of coal required. That would give him a jump on this year's requests.

He was lost in the future, picturing the children on Christmas morning, the looks of delight on their faces when they saw the presents, and the proud parents watching with contented smiles.

The weather change took him by surprise.

A gust rocked the sleigh, tearing at the pages in his hand. Shoving the list in his pocket, he increased tension on the lines leading to his reindeer. A second blast hit, rocking his vehicle, forcing him to grab the side to steady himself.

"Looks like we're into some weather," he called to the team. "Stay on course. Everything will be fine."

The wind shrieked and rain slammed into Santa, soaking and chilling him. He wore jeans, a shirt, boots, and a denim jacket rather than his familiar red furs. A western hat sat low over his eyes.

"Hold tight, Dasher. Hold your spacing, Dancer. Easy Prancer, Vixen. Comet, Cupid, Donner, get back in line. We've been in worse. Remember the night Rudolph led us through that fog. Follow Blitzen's lead. He's holding his own. We'll be out of it soon."

A strong gust drove Blitzen sideways, snapping his harness. He spun out of control away from the sleigh, the straps of his rigging trailing behind.

"Hold your track," Santa called to the remaining seven. "Donner, take the lead." He turned toward Blitzen, who struggled against the gale. "Fight it. Get control, then make a gradual turn. We'll manage until you get back. We'll be okay."

The storm grew more intense, forcing them lower until the sleigh skimmed the treetops. Donner flew as hard as he could, trying to maintain altitude, but the relentless wind shoved him, the rest of the team, and the sled downward. A runner hooked a tree limb.

The sled's abrupt stop in the top of the tree sent Santa tumbling through the branches, banging first into one then another. He never saw the sleigh separate from the reindeer and come to rest on a cushion of branches high in the air. His team, still harnessed together except for Blitzen, pawed wildly, but could gain no hold as they slowly fell behind him.

Blitzen struggled against the wind, his eyes wild, watching the catastrophe. "I must get back to Santa," he moaned.

* * *

As Santa's woes worsened above him, Sean lay with his eyes closed and his legs and arms wrapped around the tree root. Leaves, vines, and other debris, whipped by the wind, peppered him while small twigs and leaves fell on him. "Oh, this is terrible," he moaned. "I'm too young to die. I need to make arrangements for my gold and my family." A limb landed beside him, its branches raking his head. He squeezed his eyelids tighter.

A heavy object landed, shaking the ground. "That must have been a big piece of sky," Sean moaned. "Or maybe a tree. Maybe a pot of gold. Or, I could be dead." He peeked through one partially opened eye, and saw a large fat man with a white beard and white hair. "That doesn't look like Saint Peter." The leprechaun jumped to his feet and dashed several steps away. He looked back and saw the man not moving.

The reindeer settled, encircling Sean, their antlers, heads, and legs twisted in their leather trappings.

His thoughts of flight disappeared, replaced by leprechaun-dread. *My gold. One of those animals landed on my gold.* He danced back and forth, wanting to run, but afraid he'd lose his fortune.

The storm eased, leaving only a gentle rain.

The reindeer struggled to the bearded person and licked his face. They made mewling sounds, almost like baby kittens, large tears rolling from their eyes.

Sean quit skittering around and stared. Those strange animals with their antlers looked like they were crying over the man. One of them stood on his pot of gold. He stepped toward them. "Is he alright? Maybe you should move him closer to the tree." Anything to get them away from his crock.

The reindeer looked at him. One of them said, "Who are you? Can you help us?"

Sean stared at the spot where he'd buried the crock. Was that a section of the rim showing? "No way. I want you out of here. I'm Sean O'Cleary, and you're trespassing in O'Cleary Wood. And this is the O'Cleary Tree. Pack him up and leave." He pushed up onto his toes and glared at the animal who'd spoken.

"You're a mean man," the animal said. "Can't you see he's hurt and unconscious? Do you know who—"

There was a huge crash beside Sean. He spun and saw a large battered sleigh. Sean ran several steps away, then stopped, staring at the twisted carriage.

The animals stood in a protective circle around the man.

Sean walked to the animal. "Hey, what's going on here? What are you guys trying to pull? Get out of here, this is my area."

"We can't," another of the animals said. "The sleigh is busted. Our master is hurt. Won't you help us?"

"Forget it. I have my own problems, and you're in my way. The sooner you're gone, the sooner I can take care of my go . . . uh, my business."

"You're a terrible little man. My name is Donner, one of Santa's reindeer. The storm knocked us down, and Santa is injured. If you don't help us, children around the world will miss Christmas. What kind of little person are you who could let that happen?"

"I don't believe you," Sean said, distrust dripping from his words. "You're here to steal my gold. Your tricks won't work. I hid it a long way from here."

"Please, Mister. Santa Claus is unconscious. We must find a doctor for him, but our harness keeps us from moving." He shook himself and dug at the straps with his antlers to no avail. "You're the only one who can help."

Sean looked at the old man, remembering stories his father told him when he was a child. His face softened. He remembered sitting in his dad's lap and listening to the stories about a fat man with a snow-white beard who lived at the North Pole, who distributed toys to children around the world on Christmas Eve. Could it be? Nah. He'd quit believing that hogwash years before. Just a bunch of malarkey. There was no such man.

He cocked his head at the strange animal, thinking, There might be some money to be made here though. "If I bring a doctor, what's in it for me?"

The animals looked from one to another. Donner said, "We can only promise you that Santa will never forget. You'll be blessed for the rest of your life."

"Big deal," Sean said. He looked at the fat man again, then eyed the spot where he'd covered his crock. It appeared well-hidden, only small trickles of water moving around the mound. The piece of the rim he thought he'd seen was only a gold-colored leaf stuck in the ground. "Let me free you and the others before you hurt yourselves." He pulled a homemade knife from his belt and sliced at the rigging. After a few minutes of cutting, untwisting, and untangling, he had the harness removed from each of the reindeer.

"Thank you," Donner said. "Now help Santa. Please help him."

Blitzen glided to the ground beside the rest of the team, his gear trailing like ribbons on a Christmas package. "Is everyone all right? I had a terrible time with the wind and the storm, then I had to find you." He looked around and his mouth fell open. "Santa. What's wrong with Santa?"

"Another one," Sean mumbled. "Soon the woods will be full. The sooner I get them out of here, the better." To the animals, he said, "Okay, you stay here. I'll get the sawbones. Don't mess with anything. Especially, no digging."

Sean dashed along a dirt path, dodging around trees, shrubs, and puddles until he reached the leprechaun village. He came to a sliding halt in the mud of the Community Square. Debris from the storm littered the area, and there was no one in sight. He climbed onto the speaker's platform and rang the assembly bell, shouting, "Come out, come out wherever you are."

Mayor Fegan stepped from the official residence, the Bark House, built into the largest tree in the village. "What's the noise? Oh, it's you, Sean. Quit clanging that bell. What are you screaming about? Were you hurt in the storm?"

Sean slapped the bell again. "There's a guy hurt in O'Cleary wood. He needs us. His animals say he's Santa."

"Santa who? We have no one named Santa. Is this another of your jokes? If it is—"

"No. I'm not joking. The one called Donner said he's Santa Claus." Sean jumped from the dais and grabbed the mayor's arm. "His sled crashed. The animals are alright, but he's injured. Get everybody. Where's the doctor?" Sean ran in little circles looking in all directions, his words firing like machine gun bullets. Thoughts of his gold buried under the hooves of those animals drove him.

"Slow down," The mayor said. "This better be real, or it's the stocks for you."

Other leprechauns gathered around. They looked at Sean, pointed, and grinned. They knew how greedy he was, the tricks he pulled. After the last one, when he claimed he found a riverbed of gold and tried to sell shares, the Village Council sentenced him to two days punishment.

"Hey, Sean, has it been raining gold and silver?" called one. "You selling deeds?"

"Probably diamonds and pearls," another said through laughter.

Sean gazed around the gathering, then at the mayor. "Please, believe me. This is real . . . honest. I have to get back. My—" He stopped himself. He couldn't trust his neighbors.

The mayor eyed Sean, the men who were still coming from their tree homes, then Sean again. "Okay, but you'd better not be lying."

"Better be right," the others echoed.

"Remember what I said. A week in the stocks if this is one of your schemes. You five men, follow us," the mayor harrumphed.

Sean retraced his route as fast as he could. He fumed while waiting for the others to catch up. "Hurry. You walk like a bunch of human old ladies. Santa is waiting."

"So you say," Mayor Fegan said, wiping his brow. "And he'd better be there."

Sean ran to the old oak and stopped. He panted while looking along his back trail. "Hurry," he called again.

Mayor Fegan strutted to Sean's side followed by the others. "He looks a bit like Santa Claus," Mayor Fegan said, staring at the man on the ground. "Beard fits. Big belly. Clothes are all wrong though." He leaned over. "Are you okay, sir?"

"I'm all right," Santa said, rubbing his head. I have a lump on my noggin the size of a large snowball and a pain that makes me dizzy. I think my right arm is broken."

The reindeer, who stood around Santa, groaned.

He looked at the mayor. "Who are you? Where am I? Who are all these little people?" He paused, squinted, then smiled a huge Santa-smile. "You're the wee people, leprechauns. Yes, I was flying over Ireland."

"Your arm?" Blitzen said, interrupting. "How will you finish the toys?"

"We'll find a way. We must find a way. The children depend on us." He sat up and gazed around. "How's the sleigh? Will it fly?"

Sean had moved so he stood over his pot of gold, which put him beside the sleigh. "Busted. Both runners are broken and the tree branches punched holes in the sides and the cushions. That's all I see, but there may be more."

Blitzen lowered his head. "It's all my fault. I'm sorry, Santa. If only my harness hadn't broken and—"

"Nonsense, it was no one's fault," Santa said, then paused. "Well, maybe mine. I should have watched the weather." He twisted toward the sled. "Ouch. Is one of you a doctor? Can you fix my arm?"

A small figure stepped forward. "I'm Dr. O'Malley."

"Excuse me," the mayor said, pushing in front of the doctor. "Sean believes you are Santa Claus. Are you?"

"Of course he is," Blitzen said. "Are you blind?"

"Ho, ho, ho," Santa said. "It's okay, Blitzen. Many people have difficulty believing in me. Are you one of those, Mayor?"

"Well . . . ah . . . I used to."

"Give me a moment," Santa said. "My memory is not what it used to be, but I believe you received a new crock for your pot of gold last year. Am I right?" He paused. "Oh. And the milk you left out was sour."

The Mayor blushed. "I believe you." He turned to the villagers. "This man is Santa Claus. Doctor, take care of him."

A man shoved past the Mayor. "I'll say again, I'm Doctor O'Malley. It is an honor to meet you, Mr. Claus. Let me look at your arm. I'll also check that lump on your head. Mayor, get some ice. We have to keep the swelling down. Tell Nurse Shaunessy to bring my bag."

The Mayor cleared his throat. "Do I look like your errand boy? I'll send someone." He gazed at the leprechauns. "Sean, you go."

"I'd rather not," Sean said, casting glances at the small mound covering his crock. "Let someone else. I'm tired."

"Sean. You do as I say or it's the stocks with you."

He frowned, then turned to leave, but the doctor stopped him. "Better gather all the men. Have them bring the cart with the tripod, hoist, and pulley. It will take a lot of manpower to splint this arm."

* * *

While Sean dashed toward the village, the doctor examined Santa. He climbed onto a root and checked Santa's head, then

9

paced the length of his arm, a frown on his red-bearded face. Using his small hands, he felt the limb, not looking happy at all.

Santa was stoical, his face not giving anything away. "What do you think?"

"Hmmm, not good, my man, not good. Definitely broken." He continued his examination, carefully stepping over Santa's arm.

The other leprechauns milled around the sleigh and the reindeer, marveling at the damage. Ryan, the leprechaun engineer, took measurements, scratched his head, and stroked his beard while mumbling under his breath. "Never worked on anything this big. Gonna be a job, a big job."

Dr. O'Malley finished his examination, sat on a root knot, and with his hand cupping his chin, said, "Your head will be fine. Just a good bump. I'll give you something for the headache as soon as my bag arrives. The arm needs a cast. You won't be using it for a couple of months."

"Doctor, you don't understand. I am Santa Claus. There are toys to be made. Fix my arm so I can finish my Christmas orders."

"Not medically possible, my good man. Someone will have to take over for you."

"There is no one else," Santa said. A large tear dribbled from his eye and hid in his beard.

* * *

Three days passed. Santa's head was better, but he felt worse. Dr. O'Malley's medicine appeared to be helping everything except Santa's disposition. He was anxious to get home to the North Pole. Although he sent Mrs. Claus messages by telepathy that things were fine, he knew she worried. She was accustomed to his being gone, but he'd never stayed away this long before.

His arm swelled badly the first two days causing Dr. O'Malley and his team of leprechaun assistants to adjust the straps on the splint, then re-tighten them as the swelling subsided.

On the fourth day, Santa said, "No more of your tree-bark potions." He pushed away the shovel full of the brown liquid. "Enough of that stuff already. I'd rather hurt." His attitude was deteriorating although everyone knew he could never be really grumpy.

The reindeer, all except Blitzen, had scratches and minor cuts from tumbling through the tree. Dr. O'Malley and Nurse Shaunessey used healing salves for their injuries.

Blitzen's damage was to his coat. The wind had blown against it so hard the hair refused to lie down. Brenda, Sean's wife, brushed, combed, and rubbed owl fat into it until she tamed it.

On the sixth day, Dr. O'Malley decreed that Santa's arm had stabilized enough for a cast. He and seven other leprechauns mixed a large batch of plaster of Paris. After much sweating and swearing by the workmen, Santa's arm was immobilized.

"Can you free my fingers?" Santa asked. "I can barely move them. It will be impossible to finish my toy orders."

"Sorry," the doctor said. "The bone is broken. The children might be disappointed, but they'll survive. There will be no Christmas toys this year."

Santa was devastated, as were the reindeer. Blitzen took it hardest because he blamed himself for the crash. However, no amount of argument changed Dr. O'Malley's mind. He was adamant that the cast stay on for eight weeks.

The men of the village labored on the sleigh, repairing the runners, re-stitching the cushions, and reinforcing the sides. One railing had to be replaced. When repairs were complete, Santa walked around it, kicked the runners twice, then agreed it looked as good as new.

The women completed new harnesses for the reindeer, and Santa declared them works of beauty. The leather, dyed bright red with the berries of the forest, almost glowed in the dark. Every two feet, there were small silver bells.

Santa picked up the rigging. The bells tinkled with merry sounds. "Very nice," said Santa. "Much better than the old harness. Mrs. Claus will be impressed."

* * *

As the people of the leprechaun village pitched in, doing what they could to help Santa and the reindeer recover, Sean watched and listened. He marveled at them, wondering why they were being so nice to the fat old man. Oh sure, he said he was Santa, but was he? Was he really? Sean wasn't convinced. He could be just a cleaver ruse to steal all the gold in the village. Well, he wouldn't get Sean's. Not a chance. Sean would keep his hidden in his special places. So, as others worked, Sean continued his suspicious ways, moving his crock daily.

Yet, no matter how hard he fought it, there was something about the man and his animals. A feeling of good will seemed to form an aura around him. Even Mayor Fegan's sarcastic manner lessened, changing to one filled with friendliness. He clapped the men on the back and kissed the hands of the ladies, smiling all the time.

Sean's wife, Brenda, spoke of the old fat man as if he were the one and only Santa. She berated Sean for not jumping in and working with the others to fix the sleigh. She said he should be grateful the village had such a visitor, even if it took a storm to cause it.

The more Sean watched, the more uncertain he became. Was there really a Santa Claus? Was this jolly fat man the real Santa Claus? Sean's trips into the woods became shorter as he spent more time spying and trying to comprehend the changes he saw in his fellow leprechauns and the changes he felt taking place in himself.

* * *

On the tenth day, Santa spoke to the reindeer. "The sleigh is finished, your new harnesses are ready, and my arm is as good as it will be for several weeks. It is time for us to leave."

The reindeer cheered. They liked the little people, but there was no place like home.

Mayor Fegan assembled the villagers in the Community Square. "Santa has announced he will leave our village," he boomed. "We must wish him a fond farewell and a bon voyage." He stepped aside.

The crowd applauded.

"My little friends," Santa said, taking over the podium. "I can never thank you enough. If Sean had not been there, everything might have been lost." He turned toward Doctor O'Malley. "Sir, I'll never forget you for treating my head wound and my arm— even if you did make me drink that terrible tasting tree-bark stuff."

Everyone laughed and cheered.

As the noise died, someone yelled, "I put lots of honey in mine. Only way I can drink it."

The laughter sounded again.

Santa continued. "A special thanks to the beautiful ladies. Never have my reindeer looked better. And the rest of you—well, I do believe my sleigh is in better shape than ever before. But the time has come for us to leave. The first person I saw when my eyes opened was my dear friend, Sean." He paused. "Sean, would you help the reindeer into their new harnesses?" Santa looked around the crowd.

No one stepped forward.

"Sean?" Blitzen said. "Has anyone seen Sean?"

"Not I," answered Donner. "Not since last night."

"Nor I," said Cupid.

"Bet he's looking for gold," a voice called.

"Yeah. In a golden riverbed," another said.

"Or maybe the end of the rainbow."

The crowd roared with laughter.

"Quiet," Mayor Fegan called in his official voice. "We need someone to find him."

"We'll all look," Dr. O'Malley said. "He's probably moving his crock again. He worries about it all the time."

The leprechauns spread out into the forest. A few minutes later, they were back, Sean and a group of his friends with them. Each carried a large pack on his back.

"Have you found another treasure?" Mayor Fegan asked, a twinkle in his eye.

"No. I'm going with Santa."

"And I," Brenda, Sean's wife, chimed in.

Soon, twelve leprechauns, six men and six women, had announced they were leaving with Santa. Among them, there were fifteen children.

"Thank you," Santa said, "but I cannot allow it. It's too much of a sacrifice."

"We talked it over. Our minds are made up," Sean said. "Someone must finish the toys.

We'll go with you, complete them, then you can drop us off when you return Christmas Eve."

"Why, yes," Santa said. "Maybe—"

"That's a wonderful idea," Mayor Fegan said. "But, like most of your ideas, Sean, it won't work. Once you leave Ireland, you will lose your powers and your pots of gold. You'll become normal elves. You can't come home again."

O'Hannity, who stood beside Sean, said, "We know that, sir. Sean was the only one who didn't believe we'd lose our magic. Doesn't matter though. We will not allow children to be disappointed. We'll give our gold to Doctor O'Malley for a hospital. We won't need it. We'll be richer with the happiness little children provide."

The villagers looked at one another then turned away, tears leaking from eyes. The generosity of Sean and his group caught them by surprise. Who would have thought the village prankster would make the ultimate leprechaun sacrifice?

Santa sniffled, then blew his nose into a big red handkerchief. The reindeer ducked their heads lest their tears be seen.

"Thank you," Santa said after another snuffle. "I won't deny I need help. I'll find a way to make it up to you. I have certain powers. We'll see how much I can transfer."

A half-hour later, the sleigh was loaded with Sean, his friends, and their possessions. The reindeer were in their new harnesses, and Santa sat with the reins in his hand.

"Ring the bells," shouted a small child.

"Yes," called Santa to the reindeer, "make the bells jingle."

The reindeer stamped their feet and tossed their heads.

"Listen, Mother," said the little girl. "Listen to the bells." In a singsong voice, she said, "Jingle bells, jingle bells."

Santa tapped the lines lightly across the rumps of the animals. "Go Dasher, Dancer, Prancer and Vixen. Up Comet, Cupid, Donner and Blitzen. To the top of the trees, to the tip of the sky, now fly away, fly away, we must say good-bye."

With that, the reindeer lunged upward and the sleigh lifted. The villagers heard Santa exclaim as he drove out of sight, "From this day forward, Elves will save Christmas Eve night."

THE BEGINNING

AUTHOR COMMENT: Hope you enjoyed learning the background of Santa's elves. Now, we jump a few hundred years and meet Jingle Bell.

JINGLE AND JAKE

The name is Bell. Jingle . . . Bell. And no tittering. My mother named me. Her name was Sleigh. My father was Silver.

I'm a S.I. That's Santa Investigator for you less enlightened humans. How do you think the big guy sorts out the naughty from the nice—a Ouija board? No way. He needs help and he only depends on his best. I'm one of those—top of the line SI.

We keep our ears open, tuned to the children around the world. When an act is committed that could cause someone to change lists—Nice to Naughty, or better yet, Naughty to Nice, Santa tells the Santa Investigator in Charge—S.I.I.C.— and he dispatches an Assistant S.I. to check it out. I catch the toughest cases because I'm the best.

It was December tenth when the big guy called me in.

"Jingle, I have a report of serious misconduct. The S.I.I.C. is on assignment, so I'm giving this one to you."

I smiled. Just what I needed. The last months had been hectic, and we had spent most of our time on the road. The fall is always the busiest time for us—so many kids to check out.

"Rudolph had the antenna duty this morning and picked up a transmission from Texas." He tapped the world map that covers his wall. "Right here between Fort Worth and Abilene. Town named Cisco. Nice place. I've been going there for years."

"Santa," I said, suppressing a smile, "you've been going to all the towns for years."

"Well . . . ah . . . yes." He cleared his throat. "But I like Cisco."

I wanted to tell him he liked all the towns and all the cities, but decided to let it ride. I was more interested in what Rudolph reported. Since he gained fame on that *foggy Christmas Eve*, he was prone to embellishing his stories. "What did he come up with and how good is the info?"

"Said it came in crystal clear. He has an exceptional set of antlers. Perfect antennae."

Yeah, right, I thought. If I had my way, that perfect rack would hang over my fireplace.

"Yes sir." I rolled my eyes, hoping he'd move on. The old man couldn't get over Rudolph saving his deliveries that *foggy Christmas Eve*. Someone even wrote a song about it. I walked to the hassock in front of Santa's lounger, climbed up, and sat. All the chairs in his private quarters were too big. They made me feel swallowed—a Jonah and the whale complex, I suppose.

"Yes," he said. "I well remember that foggy Christmas Eve when—"

"Sir? I should get on this while the trail is warm. Sounds like a kid might be changing lists." Actually, I had no idea, but I'd heard the Rudolph story too many times. Plus, I had to get Santa back on track.

"Of course," Santa said. "Yes, this is serious. Vandalism of public property. And not just vandalism, but depriving children of their enjoyment."

He paced in a circle, clearly agitated, stroking his beard. That was my signal this one was hot.

He stopped and fixed me in a stare. "Jingle, I want you to personally handle this one. I am very upset."

"But, sir, I have—"

"Jingle Silver Bell."

That was my clue to listen and agree. When he used my middle name, he wasn't open to discussion.

* * *

I returned to my quarters to pack for the trip and to change clothes. The weather in Texas in December was a bit different from the North Pole. I put on jeans and a white polo shirt. And of course, a pair of fine Texas boots. Starting out the door, I stopped and stared at my reflection. The S.I.I.C. hung mirrors beside the exit so the last thing an Assistant S.I. saw was himself. That reinforced he'd better look good. We represented Santa, and that was serious business.

My bright red beard hung mid-chest. "Hmmmm, think I'll do the Hollywood thing to blend in." I returned to my dresser, picked up my clipper, and cut the beard off, leaving the equivalent of a human's three-day growth. You know, that grungy look popular on TV and in the movies. Then I stuffed my red hair under a classy Western hat, grabbed my favorite leather coat, and walked out the door, exaggerating my swagger to make up for the lack of six-guns by my side. Okay, that might be a bit much, but I was ready to get the truth and make the hard call on whether to switch some kid from the Nice List to the Naughty List. I have a low tolerance for misbehavior.

* * *

I banged onto the limb of a large oak. I hated it when something got in the way as I transported. Plotting coordinates didn't always take into consideration the vegetation in the area. I had to grab onto the trunk to keep from falling. Rubbing my rear end—it was a hard landing—I looked around. Yeah, it was the right place. And I was doubly sure when I saw swing frames with no children enjoying them. Short sections of rope hung from the overheads. Santa told me Rudolph's report was that someone, probably a kid, cut the ropes. My job was to find the culprit, and if he was on Santa's list, make the right call. I smiled. "Get ready, kid, a lump of coal is coming your way."

"Hey, Mac. Find your own limb. This one's mine."

I felt a nudging against my hip and saw a gray squirrel pushing against me.

"Move on. You're keeping me from my cache."

18

Although the voice was squeaky, it sounded like a poor Marlon Brando imitation. When I looked, I saw why. She had an acorn stuffed in her jaw.

"Excuse me, Ms. Squirrel," I said. "I misjudged—"

"Ms.? Buddy, you'd better get your eyes checked. Now get out of my way. I got work to do."

"Sorry." I felt myself flush in embarrassment. With a name like Jingle, I knew how having your gender confused felt—not reassuring. "We don't have many squirrels at the North Pole. I shouldn't have spoken in haste."

"I don't care—fast or slow. Just move it."

I stood, and he scooted around my feet into a knothole. When he emerged a moment later, the acorn was gone. He stopped and rubbed his jaw. "Whew. That was a big one. Had trouble getting it out past my teeth." He eyed me. "What are you doing here?"

"Do you know who I am?"

"What, you think I'm stupid? I've been outwitting cats and kids for four years. You're an elf. Dressed funny though."

I checked my Western attire. "What do you mean?"

"You gotta be a tourist. Boots and hats are out. Most folks just wear a gimme cap and sneakers."

"Oh."

"So, why are you here?"

I explained my mission.

He sat back and gazed at me as if trying to make a decision. "Yeah, you look honest enough. My name's Squiggly, Squiggly Squirrel. What's yours?"

I hesitated. Usually, when I tell someone my name, I get that look. You know, the one that says, *You gotta be kidding.* But Squiggly might be in a position to help. I had to tell him something, and if I lied, and Santa found out, he'd demote me to putting wheels on toy cars. "Jingle Bell."

A smile jumped to his squirrelly lips, showing his buckteeth. "Yeah, that fits."

I chose to ignore his remark. Tying his tail in a knot wouldn't speed my investigation. "Can you help me? Did you see who cut the ropes?"

"Of course. Who do you think keeps things under control around here? The humans don't have a clue."

"Well?"

"Well what?"

"Who was it?"

"A kid."

"And?"

"And what?"

I looked around, then settled into a sitting position on the branch. Maybe my height had him confused. "Who's the kid?"

"Beats me."

I ran my hand over my face. I felt like I was in a Bud Abbott—Lou Costello skit, and I had Lou's part. You know, the *Who's on First* routine. "Squiggly, if you saw him, and you keep watch on things around here, what's his name?"

"Beats me."

"You mean his name is Beats Me?"

"Beats me."

I stared at him. If I saw the slightest smirk, I'd vaporize his acorns. He wore a serious expression—well, as serious as a squirrel can have. "Let me try again. Do you know the young man's name?"

"Nope."

"Why not?"

"I'm a squirrel. All humans look alike to me. Who pays attention to names? Just one of the kids who throws rocks."

I digested what he said. Yeah, I could identify with it. All squirrels looked alike to me—furry with a bushy tail—and I hadn't known they had names until Squiggly introduced himself. "Tell me about that day. I'm a highly trained Santa Investigator. Maybe I'll find a clue."

"Oh, man. You better put in a good word to Santa. I still have acorns to gather."

I glared at him.

Squiggly eyed me, then grinned. "For an elf, you don't have much patience. You sure you work for Santa?"

"I know magic. I can turn your hoard of acorns into an owl. Would you like to have an owl in your knothole?"

He recoiled. "No, please don't. I'll cooperate." Under his breath, he muttered, "A guy can't have any fun these days."

"Spill it," I said.

"Two youngsters came to the park tossing a football. One of them called himself the quarterback, whatever that means, and told the other to go out for passes. Has something to do with the game they play on Friday nights at the school. People get so excited screaming at one group knocking down another group, they dump whole bags of popcorn. What a feast? And the fools just keep yelling. They don't realize the treasure trove they're giving me."

My curiosity popped up. "Tell me about it. What do they do?"

"I should know? They run, they get knocked down, then everybody jumps on. They get up, rest, then do it all over again. Sometimes they throw the ball, then run until someone trips, and everyone piles on."

"That's it. Just throw, run, trip, and jump on?"

"That's all I see. Wait, sometimes one of them kicks the ball before they run, trip, jump on."

I shook my head, trying to picture what he described. Nope, made no sense to me. "Okay, back to the day the ropes were cut."

"Yeah. Like I said, two of them were here throwing the ball. Then one left—the one without the ball. The other stayed. He walked to the swing, gave it a push, then walked away and threw the ball." He looked puzzled. "I think he was trying to get it between the ropes. When it went through, he was happy, and when it didn't, he said . . . Well, I won't repeat it. You might tell Santa."

I looked at my *Rudolph the Red Nosed Reindeer* watch—a gift Santa insisted I wear. "Can you move on? Time is flying, and I hope to get home tonight."

"Okay, but you really know how to mess up a story. Like I said, he'd give the swing a shove, then throw. Shove, throw. Shove, throw. After one miss, he ran toward the swing and kicked at it." Squiggly laughed, a high, piercing cackle. "He missed and jerked himself right off his feet, landing on his butt."

"Your squeaky laughter sounds like an owl summons."

He stopped mid-giggle.

"Go on. What happened after he fell?"

"He got up cussing. He said words I never heard before, not even from the cowboys who come here on Saturday night to drink beer.

Next thing I knew, he had a knife and was sawing at the ropes. He cut every one of them, then picked up the ball and walked away, whistling."

"And you don't know his name?" I said, hoping he'd change what he said earlier.

"Nope." He paused, appearing to think. "When they're throwing rocks, he's the one who comes closest to me. Of course, I'm too fast for any human. Does that help?"

"Not unless I get all the children in Cisco to come out and throw at you. Would you like that?"

"No way. Now, I've wasted enough time. I have work to do." He scurried away, leaping from limb to limb until he jumped onto the ground. Last I saw, he was under another oak, pushing acorns into a pile.

I leaned against the trunk, thinking about what I'd learned. Quarterback and football. Maybe that was my clue. If I did a low-level over Cisco, I might get lucky. That's what I did, and how I spotted a group of boys playing.

I dropped into the middle of their game, but remained invisible. Watching without being seen seemed like the best way to find out what was happening. After almost getting run over a couple of times, I shifted to the outside. From what I could understand, they called it practicing. They'd stop, assume funny positions, then one of them would yell, "Hut, hut, hut," and they'd take off in different directions. The one who called out the huts would throw the ball to another player. If he caught it, everyone cheered. If not, they booed.

My break came when the one who missed the ball said, "Jake Adams, you stink. We need a new quarterback."

I stared at the thrower. Had to be my man and now I had a name. He didn't look very sinister. About ten years old, towheaded, and thin. The only thing making him stand out from the others were his clothes. Expensive and they looked new.

I hung around, waiting for them to disperse. They played until darkness swamped the area. The one named Jake picked up the ball and walked away alone. Perfect.

I followed until we were out of sight of the others, then materialized beside him. "Hey, Jake, we need to talk."

He jumped. "Who are you? Where'd you come from?"

I must have scared him. I tend to forget that humans are skittish. "Take it easy. I'm harmless. Just an S.I. out on a job."

"What's an S.I.? You're too little to do much."

"Tact is not your long suit, is it? Forget I said it. Let's sit on the grass, and you tell me why you cut the ropes on the swings."

He jumped again and started to run. His mistake that time. I pointed and levitated him back, settling him beside me. "Now that's better. Just sit there."

"I'll tell my father. You'll be in trouble."

"Oh, yeah. I can see that now. You tell him one of Santa's investigators stopped you on the street to ask why you vandalized the swings in the park. Two problems with that. First, he won't believe you talked to an elf, especially one named Jingle Bell. Second, he'll be thrilled to know his son broke the law. Think about it." I paused, watching a variety of expressions cross his face.

"Wasn't me."

"Uh-huh. Denying it, eh? Just what I expect from someone who's about to move to the Naughty List. You'll have to do better than that."

"No, you can't do that to me." He clenched his fists and stood up. "You don't know who—"

"Sit down, son, or I'll sit you down."

"No way."

His defiance changed fast when his butt did a triple-bounce hitting the ground. I could have been gentler, but chose not to. He had it coming.

"Don't hurt me, sir. I'll talk to you."

"Excellent. Start with the swings."

Jake's eyes went glassy, then changed to a look of shrewdness. "I know I should have told the police, but I didn't want to get him in trouble. He comes from a poor family and has to work."

"I see," I said, not believing a word. I wanted to see how far he'd go.

"Yes, sir. I told him not to do it, but he was mad because he's not a good football player and won't make first string in high school. So . . . he cut the ropes."

"What's his name?"

"Do I have to tell you? I mean, he's okay . . . really. I'll make sure he doesn't do it again."

"Name?"

He looked away, then in a quiet voice, said, "Arty Edwards. I can show you where he lives."

I opened my notebook and scribbled the name. Then I flipped the page. "Hmmmmm, let me see." While the boys played their silly game, I accessed the Santa computer. "You're Jake Adams. Your father is the richest man in town, probably in Eastland County. No brothers or sisters. You asked for a red Schwinn bicycle with all the trimmings for Christmas." I gave him my special look. "You know, if I move you to the Naughty List, you won't get the bike . . . or anything else."

"It wasn't me. I told you."

"Yeah, I remember. First, let me check something. Look into my eyes."

He did, and I did a video search of his memory. There it was, just as Squiggly described. First, throwing at the swings, then getting mad when he missed, followed by cutting the ropes. I stood, brushing the seat of my jeans. "Let's talk to Ace."

His face said I surprised him. "Ace? Do you know him?"

"Of course. I know all the children Santa visits—and that's all the children in the world." I opened my notebook again. "Ace Edwards. That's Arthur Conan Edwards, named by his dad who owns and operates a local drugstore. Ace's mom calls him by a pet name, Arty. You heard her, and now you use it to embarrass him. They're not poor, but they're not as rich as your family." I paused and turned the page. "Anything else you want to know?" I waited a couple of beats. "Okay, on your feet, and let's go."

Jake's head was down as he stood. I took a few steps, but he didn't follow.

"What is it? Not willing to face him?"

"I . . . I might have been wrong." His voice quivered. "It might not have been Ace."

I walked back to him. "Really? If not, who was it?"

His eyes looked like two butterflies on a breezy day, flitting first one way, then another, obviously looking for another lie, but not finding it. I could have put him in a truth-trance, but chose not to. It was important he tell me on his own. I continued to stare.

"Sir?"

I waited.

"I did it."

I waited.

A total confession spewed forth, including the part about blaming Ace. Tears welled in his eyes, then trickled down his cheeks. I kept quiet, knowing my lack of comments would keep him going. He even threw in a couple of extras. And he kept repeating how sorry he was for what he did.

After he'd talked himself out, I said, "Jake, I hope you feel better after confessing. They say confession is good for the soul. I know it wins points with Santa. I report to him, and unless you convince me otherwise, I'll recommend the Naughty List."

The tears poured. He was a broken boy, wailing like a three-year old. My heart swelled, blotting out the logic and the rules my brain worked to apply. When he said, "Isn't there anything I can do?" I wilted. I might talk tough, but inside, I'm a marshmallow. Watching a ten-year-old's heart dissolve through his eyes was not my idea of fun.

"Let's think for a moment," I said. "What can you do?"

"I could raid my piggy bank and buy ropes to fix the swings."

"A good start."

He looked around, appearing frantic to please me. "Suppose I bought the ropes, then got the gang together to hang them?" He paused, a look of pleasure overtaking him. "No, no. I'll buy chains. That's it. If we use chains, no one can cut them. I have the money, and I know the hardware store has chains."

"Good," I said, proud as a new father at how he was coming around. "What about the squirrels and other animals you and your friends taunt and throw rocks at?"

"No more, sir. I'll ask my dad to put up bird and squirrel feeders. And I'll tell the guys to never do it again."

"Better. Anything else?"

"Ah . . . ah, I can't think of anything."

"What about Ace? Suppose I had believed you? Don't you owe him?"

He looked down as if studying his toes. "What can I do? Is there something I can buy him to make it right? I'll do whatever you say."

I rubbed my hand through the stubble prickling my face. How did the Hollywood types tolerate it? An idea formed. "Anything?"

"Yes sir."

"Okay, here it is. For as long as you live, I want you to help him, and do it so he doesn't know. No matter where he is or what he's doing, you keep up with him and step in whenever you can."

"I don't understand," he said, a puzzled look on his face. "How can I do that?"

"That's what you have to figure out. And if I ever think you're not trying, off to the Naughty List. No matter how old you are, I'll be watching."

"You mean, like helping him make the football team?"

"Yes, that's a good example."

He grinned. "I can do that. Will that keep me on the Nice List? Will I get my bike for Christmas?"

"No promises. But as long as you hold up your end, I'll do what I can."

"Thank you, Jingle, thank you."

The smile that creased his face was beautiful. It carried joy, the giving spirit, and love of fellow man. At that moment, Jake personified the Spirit of Christmas. I was proud of my part in changing him.

Closing case file as Jingle Bell, S.I.

THE END

27

AUTHOR COMMENT: Don't want you thinking Jingle's life is all work and no play. Sometimes, Santa sends him on vacation. Sometimes, strange things happen when he's on vacation.

JINGLE'S VACATION

I had barely rammed my toes into the warm sand of the South Florida beach when I heard the scream. Searching for the source, I saw a bikini-clad beauty pointing and heard her yell, "Stop him. He stole my purse." Her finger was directed at the back of a man racing away, sand spraying from his flying feet.

I leaped into action and dashed after him. That proved as stupid as it sounds since one of his strides equaled four or five of mine. As he dodged in and out of the crowd along the boardwalk, threatening to lose me behind the weight-challenged tourists, I knew I had to step it up a notch.

I de-materialized, transported, then dropped down in front of him. "Stop, thief," I said, holding up my hand in imitation of a traffic cop. Either he didn't see me, or he didn't find me a threat because he charged on, knocking me backward with such force my butt dug a furrow, filling my jeans with sand. That reminded me I hadn't taken time to switch to my bathing trunks. Probably a good thing since they might have been jerked down.

There is an old saw in Santa Land, *Don't make Jingle mad.* Even Santa says it with awe. The adage is based in truth. While ninety-nine percent of the time, I'm an easy going, fun loving elf, the other one percent I can be nasty. That purse snatcher must have never heard the saying because his actions left no doubt he didn't honor it.

I stood, shaking sand out through my pants legs, and shook my fist at his back. "The fun has only begun, my friend. Watch where you step."

Again, I vanished. This time, I landed far enough in front of him to prepare for his onslaught. As he neared, I shot a paralyzer beam at his right foot. As I expected, he screamed, stumbled, hopped a couple of times, then dived forward onto his face. It was gratifying to see his nose burrow into the sand as the stolen handbag landed a few feet away.

I figured snorting sand for the next few hours would teach him a lesson about beach behavior, so I left him lying there, uttering foul words like I hadn't heard since attending a professional hockey game. I'd have stopped and added him to the Naughty List right then, but figured he probably already had a position of honor there. I could always check later.

I picked up the purse just as he let out a stream of words that startled a flock of grackles scavenging nearby. They took to the sky with angry cries at missing out on a bag of popcorn someone spilled. I glanced around the area and saw children staring at the potty-mouthed man. Too much. A quick zip of my finger and he went silent, one hand holding his foot and the other pointing to his mouth.

I set the spells for thirty minutes, figuring that was long enough to hold him until the police showed up. With him going nowhere soon, I looked up-beach for the winsome beauty who owned the bag. She was busy talking to two bicycle cops, her hands waving in my direction.

A moment later, I settled beside her and said, "Excuse me, miss. I believe this is yours." The bag I held was almost as big as me, but, being ever the gentleman, I held it up.

She jumped, then stared at me. "That's him. That's the little man who stole my bag. He ran away with it."

Now I admit I have been confused with others before. Or more correctly, I should say others have been confused with me. To most folks, all us elves look alike. So, having her say he's the one wasn't a complete surprise—at first. Then it dawned on me, she had me mixed up with someone at least six feet tall. I'm proud of my height, but two feet versus six feet should not be mistaken. I stared at her in disbelief, waiting for her to blink a couple of times and take back her identification.

One of the cops looked down and said, "Okay, kid. Give me the purse, then put your hands behind you. You know the routine." He pulled out a set of handcuffs better suited to my thighs than my wrists.

I gave him the bag, and he passed it to the lovely bikini-lady. She fumbled through it. "My sunscreen is missing. I'll get cancer. Make him tell you where it is. Make him get me another."

That did it. I'd heard it as a cliché—*there is no fiction in South Florida*—but it, like the saying about my anger, must have been based in fact. The young woman had me misidentified with someone four-feet taller, a cop wanted to handcuff me with human-sized manacles, and she, sunning herself under the hot July sun, was afraid of skin cancer. Too much. I vanished.

I didn't go far though. My curiosity about how a bicycle cop takes a suspect to jail kept me hovering close, about twenty feet off the ground. Did they handcuff the criminal to the frame and make him run alongside? Or was he expected to sit on the rear luggage carrier? Of course, the obvious would have been they called for a cruiser, but I discounted that. In all the television shows, the policeman is anxious to get credit for the collar. No TV cop was likely to allow another the opportunity to claim credit. Since none of the three arrest modes appealed to me, I decided to stay invisible and wait until they vacated the area.

Besides, I was on vacation and determined to enjoy the beach. Little things like a purse snatching and a case of mistaken identity weren't about to ruin it. Two glorious weeks of lying on the beach and watching the bikinis pass by. That was my plan. I saw no reason to change it.

In case you're wondering, I should probably explain. I'm what's commonly known as a Christmas Elf. I work for Santa, not as a toy maker, but as his S.I.I.C. That's Santa-Investigator-in-Charge. It's well-known that Santa keeps two lists, one for nice people and one for naughty ones. What doesn't get media attention is who conducts the investigations that lead to the placements. That's me. Well, me and my staff. Each year, Santa has us bouncing around the world chasing leads. Most of the time, I'm proud to say, the nice list does not shrink. But there are times I uncover behavior unbecoming a Nice and a cut has to be made. I don't enjoy it, but Santa has certain expectations. The guy I'd taken down on the beach was headed for a change, or at a minimum, a re-enforcement of his status as a baddie. He'd spend the rest of his life with nothing but chunks of coal in his stockings.

It had been a tough year, wars all around the world, petty dictators that fed off the weaknesses of their people, and the U.N. doing little to live up to its charter. Probably the worst year we'd had for folks changing lists. Seemed like civilization was moving backwards, people losing the basic courtesies which made humankind unique. I was exhausted.

Santa noticed and insisted I take a vacation. "Find a beach and lay around for a couple of weeks," he said. "Then get back here ready to work. It figures to be a busy fall."

So here I was in Hollywood, Florida in July. I had admired the boardwalk ever since Santa and I flew over it one clear Christmas Eve. The waves washing onto the beach, their phosphorescence causing them to glow as the water found its way back into the ocean were hypnotic. That night, every bar and restaurant were filled with people having a good time. I knew then I wanted to vacation there. Didn't matter what month because the weather was perfect all year round.

After Santa's declaration, I was out of Santa Land within the hour. Nobody has to hit me in the head with a toy truck to get action. But, instead of being stretched out on a towel soaking up the rays while ogling bikini beauties, I was hovering above two cops who wanted to jail me. Not my idea of a great beginning.

I looked down the boardwalk and saw the purse snatcher recovering. He was on his feet, looking at his foot. Apparently, the paralysis was wearing off. He took a couple of tentative steps, then shook the leg a few times. After that, he seemed satisfied all was well.

At first, he walked away from my position, but then he stopped and looked back. I saw him set his jaw, and he turned, increasing his stride. His face had a peculiar look, but his eyes burned into the beauty he robbed. I was mesmerized by the scene, not wanting to believe he'd be stupid enough to go after her again. That is, unless there was more to the purse snatching than met the eye. Did he know her? Was she his girlfriend? Had she wronged him in some way, and he demanded retribution? The possibilities were endless. No way I could leave.

I searched for the two policemen, but they had moved up the boardwalk, slowly peddling their way through the crowds. I could go after them, but time would be wasted. Besides, I might find myself handcuffed to their handlebars. What to do? My first day of vacation and I faced a far tougher decision that the naughty or nice list.

Only one thing I could do. Santa's code said I had to see that no harm came to a human. Ensuring that I was still invisible, I flitted to the side of the young lady. In spite of the situation, I marveled at her. We didn't have visions like her in Santa Land. And that bikini? If she bought it based on the amount of material it contained, the price must have approached free.

Too soon, my concentration was broken. The thief was within paging distance.

"Hey, you," he called. "You the one I grabbed the purse from?"

She looked around, her feet inching her backward. "It's you. I was wrong. Stay away from me. I'll scream."

"Scream all you want. But what makes you think your scream will be noticed among all the others? This is a beach. People scream all the time. You should be here in January when all the Canadians are in town. Hard to order a beer with all the noise."

"What do you want?" she said, clutching her purse to her chest. "Somebody already lost my sunscreen. I could get cancer standing here talking to you. I have no money—well, a ten-dollar bill for a bottle of water later. You want it, you can have it."

"I changed my mind. I don't want your money. But, where'd your bodyguard go? We got something to settle. He ruined my flip-flop."

"The police took him . . . well, they tried to. Then he just . . . uh, disappeared. One minute he was there, the next he was gone. Funny looking little man, wasn't he? Real short, too. He's not my bodyguard. I thought he was with you. Wonder why he took my sunscreen."

The last caused me to look up at her. Nature might have endowed her with a gorgeous body, but that didn't mean she could insult me. One more crack, and I would curl her hair—from the inside out.

"I figure he's a Canadian," tall and sinister said, his face relaxing. "They don't usually come down in July though. Probably a left-over from last season. That happens, you know. They forget to go home in April."

"It won't work," she said. "You can't soften me up that easy. You just want to steal my purse."

"Nah. I'm not in the mood anymore. I need to find that little guy. He owes me a flip-flop." He eyed her. "Where're you from?"

She shuffled her feet, like she was embarrassed. "Canada. I like the beach so I stayed. One of those who forgot to go home, I guess. My name's Cherry. What's yours?"

"Most gals call me Choco—short for Chocolate. They say it's 'cause I'm so tasty."

I groaned. Choco and Cherry? It reminded me of the commercial when peanut butter and chocolate bump together. Was I seeing the birth of a new candy bar? Santa had warned me that South Florida was unusual.

He smiled and didn't look so sinister. In fact, he looked downright nice.

Cherry must have noticed the same thing because she said, "Choco. Yeah, the name fits. You do look right tasty. Where're you from?"

He grinned. "New York. I moved here for the beach. Plus, I really hate cold weather."

I decided to enter the discussion before they started planning how many kids they'd have and what nationality they'd be. I hovered between them. "So, why'd you steal her purse?"

Both jumped when they saw me.

"There he is," Choco said. "You burned my flip-flop. You owe me a new one."

I stroked my beard. He did have a point. The one on his right foot had seen better days. One strap was loose, and there were scorch marks on the sole. "Okay, point taken," I said. "A new pair will be under your Christmas tree."

"That's six months off. I need them now."

"Yep," I said. "Looks like you do. Maybe you ought to get a job, earn some money, and buy a pair."

"I'm trying," he said. "I was laid off as a shell-stringer. Then someone stole my wallet with my credit cards, driver's license, and everything. When I reported it, the bank froze my account. I can't get any money out until Friday."

"Today is Wednesday," Cherry said. "That's, uh . . ." She counted on her fingers. ". . . two more days."

Oh, boy. The Creator must have used all his time and talent on her body. He sure forgot to fertilize the brain. I suspected it hadn't grown since birth.

"Yeah," Choco said. "And I haven't had anything to eat since yesterday morning. That's why I grabbed your purse."

"Oh, you poor dear," she said. "Here." She reached into her bag and came out with a ten-dollar bill. "Take it. I can get more. Men like to give me money."

There was no doubt in my elfin mind that she spoke the truth.

He stared at her. "I can't take your money. Not after what I did. I just want to say I'm sorry. It was a terrible thing. But when I saw your purse just lying there . . . Well, I shouldn't have done it."

"Yeah," I said. "I hope you learned your lesson."

"I promise I'll never do it again."

"Why are you wearing such funny clothes," Cherry asked, fingering my sweater. "No one else has on a shirt."

That did it. What really galled me was she was correct. My North Pole clothes were all wrong for the beach. I de-materialized and hovered above them. My first day of vacation had started on a low and slide downhill. I vowed to change into my bathing trunks before anything else happened, so I did. I asked myself what Santa would do in such a situation. The answer was obvious so I dropped into view again.

"You're back," Choco said. "And you changed outfits. With that pasty white skin, you'd better use sunscreen. Maybe Cherry will give you some."

"No, you stole it, then lost it," she said. "Don't you remember?" She pointed at me. "Or maybe he lost it. I'm confused."

She was confused? Imagine my mental state. There was no need fighting it any longer. I was the centerpiece in an Abbot and Costello skit. "If you two will be quiet a moment, I have something to say."

Both did the lock the lips and throw away the key routine. Just what I needed, vaudeville rejects. "I want to buy our reformed thief a decent meal. Would you care to join us, Cherry?"

Both of them stared at me as if I were only two feet tall. Okay, so I was only two feet tall. They still stared.

"Shall we go?" I said, taking their hands.

It was no problem leading them to the nearest restaurant. Either they were in shock, or they were in awe of me. I prefer the latter. I am a pretty intimidating guy.

After a hearty lunch for Choco and a salad for Cherry, I paid the bill, then headed next door. If they missed me, they didn't show it when I popped back in with two tubes of sunscreen. Their heads almost touched as they whispered to one another. I set one tube on the table and de-materialized, taking a quick peek into the future. I smiled, feeling like Cupid.

I settled under a palm tree for a sun-soaked nap. Before falling to sleep, I reminded myself to purge the Naughty List. Choco had made the transition.

THE END

AUTHOR COMMENT: Another episode of Jingle Bell, the Santa elf, coming your way.

JINGLE AND THE DISAPPEARING TOYS

It was January ninth, and the most exciting thing about it was there was no excitement. I leaned back in my office chair with my fine Western boots resting on the desk, sucking on a candy cane. It was as close to a down-season as we get in Santa Land. That lull before we have to get serious again. I'd given my associate investigators a month off after the busy buildup to Christmas. We were all exhausted on December twenty-sixth, and I spent most of the next week sleeping. On January second, after cleaning up from the New Year Eve's party, I sent them on their way.

Since I was alone in the office, I could dress as I pleased, rather than attempting to look like a successful elf-executive. With my boots, I wore jeans, a plaid western shirt, and my best Stetson. Of course, my silver belt buckle had the head of a longhorn embossed on it. Since I hadn't trimmed my red beard in a few days, it hung onto my chest.

A light snow with huge flakes fell outside my window effectively shutting me off from the rest of the world, making me feel like I drifted in a fluffy white cloud. My eyelids refused to stay open despite my struggle with them. If Rudolph caught me sleeping on the job, he'd run straight to Santa. He and I did not exchange gifts on Christmas morning, not since his head outgrew his antlers after he led Santa's team on that foggy Christmas Eve.

At the main house, I knew Santa and Martha were kicked back and enjoying their respite from responsibility. I pictured her sitting in her rocker, knitting as she chided him about the weight he gained from all the milk and cookies. They were a delightful couple, and I cherished them like a favorite aunt and uncle. I'd do anything for them.

Of course, my job as Santa's SII.C.—that's Santa-Investigator-in-Charge—meant I often did things he would not entrust to others. It was an awesome responsibility—investigating children around the world for list assignment, Naughty or Nice. And, while there were times when the hard call was the right one, the majority of my cases left the child on the Nice List. I much preferred that outcome.

I rose and walked to the door, opened it, and peered into the whiteness. So quiet, so peaceful. In the pasture, I saw a soft red glow—Rudolph showing off, I supposed. Reaching out, I caught several snowflakes, then tasted them—soft, moist, cold. Life was good.

Leaning against the doorframe, I conjured up an image of Santa. He'd be wearing his red pants with the white fur cuffs, black patent leather boots, a casual shirt, and his red suspenders. I suspected he might slip a nap into his early planning for next Christmas.

The intercom clicked. "Jingle. You out there?"

I hurried to my desk and pressed the *speak* button. "Yes, Santa." So much for his taking a nap.

"Get over here. We have a problem."

"Okay. Give me a—"

"Now."

"I'm halfway there as we speak."

"Then quit talking and get all the way here." Another click and silence. I listened, hoping for at least a small ho, ho, ho.

I stared at the box, then glanced at the calendar. Something important was up. Santa seldom got short with me—or anyone else. But what could it be on January ninth? Only one way to find out. I grabbed my lambskin jacket and headed for the big house.

Martha opened the door as I stepped onto the porch. "Oh, thank you for coming, Jingle. He's so upset. It's not good for his heart, you know." Her words were heavy, and her face reflected worry. Whenever Santa got edgy, her mothering genes took over.

"What is it?"

"Jingle, is that you? Quit quizzing Martha and get in here. There's a mess to be straightened out."

"Yes sir." I hustled into the main room knowing procrastination would only make my entry more contested.

I skidded to a halt in front of his chair. His face was red, redder than the ruddiness of his usual complexion. His fists clenched and relaxed, but his knuckles remained white.

"Look at this," he said, handing me a sheet of paper.

"Okay if I sit down?" I grinned, hoping to calm him a bit.

"Sit, stand, whatever. Just read. I need your opinion." He didn't smile.

I've worked for Santa a long time. I guess you could say I was born into the job. As a tot, I carried messages, then became an apprentice toymaker, toymaker, foreman, and Assistant SI before he promoted me to warehouse supervisor and stationed me in Texas. From there, after a particularly tough episode, he brought me back to Santa Investigator. I started near the bottom again, but worked my way up the chain. When Sherlock retired, I became SII.C. That had given me many years to learn to judge Santa's moods. But if I were a newbie straight from under a bridge somewhere, I would have known his mood tonight—angry, frustrated, and looking for answers.

"I'll make a nice pot of hot chocolate," Martha said, walking into the room. "I've always said, a cup of—"

"Great idea," Santa said. "But do it in the kitchen—and be slow about it."

A hurt look flicked across her face, then she smiled. "Yes, I'll add marshmallows. They're so soothing." With another troubled glance at her husband, she disappeared toward the kitchen.

"Well. You gonna read or keep staring at me?"

I looked at the paper. It was from a Mrs. Tomatra of Coral Springs, Florida.

> *Santa,*
>
> *It is difficult to write this letter because you've always been so nice to me—first, as a little girl and then, as a mother. But Georgie's heart is broken. He wrote to you asking for a new bicycle for Christmas. When he talked to your assistant at the mall, he asked again.*
>
> *But on Christmas morning, there was no bicycle. He's so disillusioned, says he doesn't believe in Santa anymore.*
>
> *What happened? Why? What can I tell him?*

It was signed, *A Former Believer.*

"Hey, you can't please everyone," I said. "We all make a mistake now and then."

"Read this one." He sailed another at me.

It was from Mrs. Lamberts in Coral Springs. The gist of it was the same except it was a pair of in-line skates missing from under the tree.

While I compared the two letters, Santa paced the room, several more papers in his hand. He stopped in front of me. "Look at these. Mrs. Nolan's granddaughter didn't get the remote-control Tinker Bell she asked for. Mrs. Fernandez' son asked for an iPad and it wasn't there."

"I don't understand," I said. "Maybe—"

"I checked, Jingle. I left every one of those gifts under the right tree. Something happened to them."

"Maybe the kids—"

Santa's glare cut me off. "I've been in this business a long time. Yes, I know children break things, then say they never got them, but this is too many from too close together. Something foul is going on in Coral Springs, something even bigger than crooked commissioners. I want to know what it is."

I swallowed. This was not going well. I'd never seen Santa so worked up.

"Hot chocolate for everyone," Martha said, entering with a tray. "I put extra marshmallows in the cups." A room-warming smile covered her face.

Santa cut her a look, but her smile never wavered. Gradually, he relaxed and even managed a small grin himself. "Martha, my dear, your hot chocolate might not cure everything, but the things it misses probably aren't worth bothering with. Jingle, looks like we have no choice but to relax and enjoy." He squeezed out a small ho, ho, ho as he gave her a look of pure love.

I couldn't help myself. I blushed bright red. Anytime I'm in the presence of people like Santa and Martha, I tend to get flustered. I keep hoping there's a lady-elf who will melt my feelings like she does his.

"Here's your cocoa," she said, handing me a cup. "And I brought some chocolate chip cookies. Santa, you can only have two. You haven't recovered from your Christmas Eve binge yet."

That forced a laugh from all of us, improving the mood of anger and frustration. We settled in front of the fireplace.

"What do you think, Jingle?" Martha asked. "Is someone stealing toys after they're delivered?"

"Looks like it," I said. "Santa, suppose I bring Flake in off vacation and have him check it out? I can have him back here by tomorrow, no later than the day after."

"No, this is your job. I can't afford any slipups."

"But, if I don't show confidence in my subordinates, how will they—"

"Jingle Silver Bell. Don't make me repeat myself."

Anytime he uses my full name, it's clearly time to say, yes sir, yes sir, three bags full, so I did. Once I accepted his ultimatum, we planned my trip. I'd leave the next day and scout around South Florida until I came up with a reasonable explanation. Then we'd figure what to do next.

I didn't mention it, but I couldn't help but wonder how someone got into the houses after Santa left. Alarms protected most homes, and it took magic to bypass them, so chances of someone stealing the toys were slim. I hoped this wasn't a sign of slippage in Santa. I couldn't bear to face such a situation. But he was several hundred years old.

* * *

The next morning, I trimmed my beard, careful to leave the faddish four-day growth look, then materialized on University Avenue in Coral Springs. I hadn't been there for a while, so I decided to use a few minutes to look around. The few, very few, pedestrians paid no attention. And the drivers simply continued to race the traffic signals.

After satisfying myself that nothing much had changed, I moved on with the idea of checking the first family on my list. However, before reappearing, I needed to change clothes. My Hawaiian shirt and neat shorts stood out like Rudolph's nose in a snow bank. An oversized, white T-shirt and baggy cargo shorts appeared to be the uniform of the day.

At the Tomatra house, I saw the expected sign proclaiming alarms protected the home. I stood in the street and thought about it, then zapped myself to the rear. Nice pool and more alarms around the doors and windows. How could someone take the toys after Santa left?

The same situation existed at the Lamberts and Fernandez houses. The only difference at the Nolans was it was a second story condo. Still nothing obvious explaining how the gifts could have disappeared.

Now that I'd checked the scene of the crime from the outside, the next step was to see inside the houses and talk to the principals. I reappeared in front of the Tomatra home and rang the doorbell.

A man opened the door. "Who . . . Alright, who's the wise guy," he said, looking around.

I tugged on his pants leg. "Down here."

"Oh, crap. Now there are midgets on my steps. If you're an exterminator, forget it, woe to the bug that crosses Betsy's path."

"No sir," I said, wondering about exterminator midgets. "I'm here for Santa in response to Ms. Tomatra's letter. Is she in?"

"Who knows? Come in and see for yourself. I'm watching sports." He walked away, leaving the door open.

I peeked inside, shrugged, and entered. First in a quiet voice, then louder, I called, "Ms. Tomatra? Are you here?"

An attractive lady entered the room wiping her hands on a dishtowel. "Who's making all that racket?" She stopped, staring at me. "You're really short."

No doubt about her vision. I figured she would have spotted the bike if it were there Christmas morning. I raised onto my toes. "I'm Jingle Bell, Santa's chief investigator. I'm here—"

"Yeah? Where's the bike?"

"We'll get to that later. Tell me about Christmas morning, the *not* finding the bike part."

"What's to tell? I looked. No bicycle. It wasn't there."

"But—"

"Georgie. Come in here. This guy needs you."

The man entered the room. "What now? You know I don't like interruptions when I'm watching a game."

"You're always watching a game," she said. "Talk to the midget."

"Elf, ma'am, elf. Not a midget. A midget is—"

"Whatever. Georgie?"

He let out a deep sigh and rolled his eyes. "Okay. I wrote Santa. I also asked one of his assistants. No one delivered. I can't get any exercise." He glared at me. "I'm going back to my game. The Swedish curling team is up by one." He stomped from the room.

"So?" Ms. Tomatra said. "Did you bring it?"

"A couple more questions," I said, thinking about how the Tomatra family would look on the naughty list. "Were your alarms set Christmas Eve?"

"Of course."

"Did you leave milk and cookies?"

"Of course."

I ran my hand over my eyebrows. She was such a talkative lady. I could barely slip in a question. "Were they gone when you got up in the morning?"

"Of course."

Okay. It was past time for a graceful exit. I was rushing to nowhere. "Thank you for your report. Rest assured, I'll get to the bottom of this." I turned toward the door.

"Aren't you going to ask about the handlebar grip?"

"Huh?"

"Well?"

I took a deep breath, considering a return to toymaker first class. "What handlebar grip?"

"The one Santa left under the tree. A terrible joke, I say."

I rubbed my temples, not surprised I had a headache forming. "Ma'am, Santa doesn't make jokes . . . well, not on Christmas Eve anyway. Are you telling me you found a handlebar grip under your tree?"

"Of course. What? You don't understand English? What do you speak at the North Pole?"

"Real English," I mumbled, then in a normal voice said, "Tell me about the grip."

"What's to tell? I came in—no bicycle, only a handlebar grip."

I scratched my stubble, wondering what happened. I knew Santa wouldn't pull a stunt like that. I mean, two hundred years is long enough to get to know someone. "Thank you," I said as she glared at me. "I'll move on now. I have other stops to make."

"Well, if that's your attitude. What about the damage to my rug?"

"Excuse me. What damage?"

"An impression, a deep one. It took two ice cubes to raise it. Whoever dropped off the bike must have put the kickstand down. It crushed the nap, and I just replaced that carpet last summer. You people should be more considerate of others' homes."

"So, you're saying the bike was here, then disappeared. Is that right?"

"Of course. Are you dense or something? What did you think happened?" She put her hands on her hips. "Now, when does Georgie get his bike?"

I wiped my forehead, damp with either sweat or frustration—or both. "Tomorrow." I hoped Santa would live up to my promise. Putting wheels on toy trucks looked better every moment.

Once out of the Tomatra house, I transported into the upper branches of a tree to think about what she'd told me. Apparently, the bike had been there. That meant someone broke in after Santa left and stole it. That same someone must have defeated the alarms. Interesting. Time to talk to the other people.

Over the next two hours, I hit the other three houses on my list—Lamberts, Nolans, and Fernandez. Better attitudes, but the stories had disturbing similarities. At the Lamberts's, an empty in-line skates box and one shoelace were found under the tree. The Nolans discovered a remote control and a picture of Tinker Bell, but no doll. An earpiece that would fit an iPad and a subscription to a music Internet site had appeared at the Fernandez's. And, to add insult to injury, at each house, the milk glass was empty and only cookie crumbs remained on the plate.

Something was amiss, but what? Was someone trying to embarrass Santa? And if so, why? Each homeowner assured me the alarms were set. This called for something stronger than pondering in a tree. This called for a latte. Or better yet, a large cappuccino with caramel and whipped cream.

I zapped myself to the nearest coffee shop and joined the line leading to the *Place Order Here* spot. An earnest, young lady dutifully took orders and called them to her co-workers as she marked cups.

The man in front of me placed his order and stepped aside. "May I help you?" the attendant said to the woman behind me.

"Excuse me, miss," I said. "I'm next."

She looked down at me. "I'm sorry. I didn't see you. You're really short."

What is it with people and their height fixations? "Or you're really tall," I said, grinning.

Ignoring my witty repartee, she said, "What can I fix for you—a mini-latte?" She giggled.

I wanted to retort, but the lady behind me cleared her throat. "Will you hurry up? I have to pick up my son. We live three blocks from the school, and he's only fifteen so he can't drive yet."

I placed my order and stepped aside, looking around for a vacant table. The inside ones were filled by people drinking coffee and plinking on computers. But that was okay with me. When the weather's right, I prefer sitting outside. Don't get much opportunity for that up north.

A second young lady served my cappuccino, and I made my way to a table in the sun. Oh, in case you're wondering, no one paid much attention to me. I'd learned from previous trips that people in South Florida seldom go eye-to-eye with anyone.

I doodled on a napkin, trying to find some logic in what I'd learned about Santa's gifts. I knew he'd made delivery, but someone or something had taken them away. Okay, simple theft I could understand, although broaching the alarms added another ingredient. But why leave evidence the gifts had been there? Strange. Very strange.

I was almost through with my coffee. Time for me to come up with my next move. But I was stumped as to what that might be. The trail was too cold to find footprints or anything else of value.

I looked at my napkin and noted the questions I'd written.

1. *How thief get in?*
2. *Why traces of gifts?*
3. *Why those gifts?*
4. *Why four houses? Were there more?*

"I can answer those."

I looked around to see who spoke. The couple at the next table had their heads together, appearing to be lost in love. Their words were for their ears only. The only other people outside were an elderly couple who looked like they never communicated with anyone, especially one another. Their heads were down as they concentrated on their drinks.

"Last first. I hit only four houses because I figured that would be enough."

The sound came at me from across the table, but there was no one there. Did I mention that South Florida can be strange?

"Who are you?" I asked. "And where are you?"

A giggle was my first answer. "You've slipped, Jingle. Or maybe my feelings should be hurt."

The voice was familiar, tugging at a memory buried in my subconscious.

"Okay. How about the answer to your second question?"

My napkin swiveled to face away from me.

"Let's see. Why traces of gifts? Simple. I wanted you here."

I frowned. "I'm here, so show yourself, whoever you are."

"There you go again. When you dumped me, I knew you didn't care about anybody but yourself. You proved it by forgetting all about me."

"What do you mean? I only—" A memory surged forward. "Hoarfrost? Is that you?"

"Bingo. Give the ugly elf with the red hair a Kewpie doll."

I watched as a face I hoped to never see again materialized across the table—my former assistant whom I chastised for Conduct Unbecoming a Santa Investigator. Specifically, I discovered he took payoffs from kids to keep them on the Nice List. When I confronted him, he admitted his violations with a smirk. I had no choice but to recommend a reduction.

"I didn't dump you," I said. "I don't know what went on between you and Santa, but I thought demotion to reindeer pen cleaner fit you perfectly. After all, you and Rudolph got along so well."

"Yeah. That's what you said. But I ran away rather than submit to such an indignity. When the old man sided with you, I told him I was outta there. Hoarfrost Rime scoops for no one."

"Okay, that's old news. What did you have to do with the toy thefts?"

"You mean the bicycle, in-line skates, Tinker Bell, and iPad? Never heard of them."

"Cute." I studied him. It had been about a year and a half since he'd left Santa's employ, and the time had not been kind to him. His hair was scraggly, needing a cut and the clothing he wore was dirty and torn. Plus, there was a distinct odor rising from him, leaving me to wonder when he last bathed. If there was such a thing as a homeless elf, I was looking at one.

I scanned the other tables and saw the older woman cast nervous glances at us. The wrinkle of her nose said her sense of smell was still young enough to notice Hoarfrost.

"Maybe we should move on," I said. "You're attracting attention. Let's go someplace we can talk in private, and you can explain what you hope to accomplish by stealing toys."

"Sure. No people sounds good to me. I know just the right spot."

He put his hand on my arm and we were soon zooming through space. When we settled, it was dark, and we were in the middle of a grove of palm trees. "Where are we?" I asked, "and what time is it?"

"Quiet Waters Park. That's in Deerfield Beach. Time? Oh, about two in the morning. I didn't think you'd mind if I jumped us ahead a bit. I don't want anyone disturbing us."

"No. Not if it'll get you talking sooner. Now, why'd you steal those toys? I have a report to write."

He laughed an elfish giggle. "You're the big boss investigator. You mean you haven't figured it out yet?"

"I'd prefer you tell me."

His response was a blow to my chest that knocked me against a palm tree. Not a jab with his fist like a human might use. A laser flash, supposed to be an elf's last line of defense.

I rubbed the spot where he'd connected, then scooted to a sitting position, leaning against the tree. "I guess Santa forgot to take away your powers."

He laughed again. This time it sounded sinister. "Yeah. Just like he forgot when he picked you to be SII.C. He forgot I was the senior investigator, and that job was mine. But after I get rid of you, he'll be only too happy to give me my due."

I stroked my chin wishing I had my beard. Stubble was for Hollywood phonies, not elves. "So this is all about revenge? You think Santa cheated you. Is that it?"

"Not Santa, you. You told him a pack of lies that made him turn against me. You lied so you could be the big man." His giggle echoed through the trees. "Big man. Get it? An elf wanting to be a big man? Can't happen."

It dawned on me that Hoarfrost might have a few Christmas ornaments loose on his tree. In fact, his lights might not run all the way to the star. "You haven't told me why you stole the toys."

"Simple. I know Santa. I knew he'd send you to find out what happened. Nothing upsets him more than kids not getting their gifts. I followed him Christmas Eve, then hit those four houses. I figured at least one of them would squawk, and you'd come along." He tapped me in the chest again. "Worked, didn't it? Here you are just like I knew you'd be."

I stood. "Yeah, I'm here. What now?"

"Simple. I'm going to dump your body on Santa's doorstep. Then he'll know who the best man is."

Wow. For the first time, I realized how serious he was. His disappointment or hatred or whatever had driven him over the edge. I was in danger—real danger. "Let's talk about this, Hoarfrost. I didn't then and don't know now why Santa picked me as SII.C. instead of you. I didn't ask for the job, and I sure didn't make up any stories about—"

Another blast from his forefinger interrupted me and my back met the tree with a thump again.

"You're lying," he screamed, his eyes flaming red. "I know what you did. You're finished."

He pointed at me, and I knew it was time to change tactics. Conversation wasn't getting me anywhere. I vanished, then reappeared behind him. "Back here, Hoarfrost. You're facing the wrong direction."

He spun and cut loose a laser beam, but I was gone before it left his fingertip. "Tsk, tsk, tsk," I said from above him in a tree. "Your reflexes aren't what they used to be."

Again, he was a moment late as a palm frond disintegrated under his flash without touching me. "Stand still and fight like an elf," he screamed. "Quit jumping around."

"You mean like this?" I said from his right side. "Or maybe this," I said landing to the left of him. "Or maybe even this." I conjured a rope and quickly looped it around him.

Alas, I wasn't fast enough. He yanked a hand free, burned through the rope and caught me with another jolt.

I landed flat on my back beside one of the trees and rolled behind it just in time to escape another flash. The tree took a terrible hit that might have finished me if he'd connected. The only way I could stop him was to hurt him, and SI's didn't do that without Santa's specific permission. Time to retreat to fight another day. I transported.

* * *

"And you're sure it was Hoarfrost?" Santa asked.

"Yes sir." Santa and I sat in front of a fire in the front room of his house where I'd briefed him on my trip to Florida. "There's no doubt about it. And," I hesitated, not wanting to say it, "he's lost it. He's not the same elf that worked for you for so many years. I feel sorry for him."

"I understand," Santa said. "But that doesn't change things. We cannot allow his shenanigans. Humans might get hurt. Bring him in."

"What will you do?" I asked. It may sound stupid after what Hoarfrost pulled, but once he was my friend. "Can you help him?"

Santa studied me for a moment. "Jingle, that's one of the reasons I picked you over Hoarfrost as my S.I.I.C. You care about people—all people. He was always cold and calculating. I knew if you recommended a child for the Naughty List, it would be after you'd exhausted every avenue to keep him clean. I couldn't depend on him for that."

I ducked my head, feeling a blush creeping up my neck. "Thank you, Santa. And yeah, I do care. Maybe too much sometime."

"Ho, ho, ho. You just keep doing what you've been doing. I'll let you know when you're wrong."

"How will you know?"

"Simple. If you save a kid by giving him a second chance, you've done the world a favor. The bad ones will show their true colors with a second offense and more. It doesn't bother me when you give the benefit of the doubt."

"But what about Hoarfrost? Do you think he can be saved?"

"I hope so." He sighed. "Bring him in, and we'll see."

I considered my last meeting with him, his out-of-control behavior. "I may need help. Do you have anything you can teach me?"

"Pick a couple of assistants to go with you, then come back here. I may have a trick or two left."

* * *

Two days later, I sat in the same coffee shop where Hoarfrost contacted me previously. If he was still in the area, I figured he'd be watching. I was almost finished with my latte when he appeared.

"Sorry to keep you waiting," he said, "but I had to neutralize your two bodyguards. It's a bit insulting that you brought two softies like them."

"What did you do?" I asked, fearing his response.

"Don't worry. They'll be okay. Maybe a bit of a headache, but that's all. However, they won't be assisting you anytime soon. Did you come back to finish what we started?"

"Yes. I spoke with Santa and he asks that you come home. He wants to help you."

He giggled in such a sinister way that a couple of snowbirds eyed him. "Oh, I will be going *home*, as you call it, but under my terms. Santa will rue the day he crossed me."

I looked around, then leaned forward. "Let's get out of here. There's no need involving humans in our problem. How about the place we went before?"

He touched my arm. "Exactly what I was thinking."

For the second time, I found myself in the dark with him amidst palm trees. "Quiet Waters Park?" I said.

"Yep, I like it here. This is where I live." He waved his arms around. "Not many people come this deep into the trees and those that do, promptly forget what they see."

"You tamper with humans? You know that's against the rules."

"Rules, smules. Who cares? Soon, you won't care either. And you won't feel so righteous."

He raised his hand and pointed his index finger at me. Before he could trigger an attack, I shot from the hip, slamming a light beam into his chest, knocking him backward against a tree.

He shook his head and stared at me. "Not bad. You're quicker than I remembered, but it won't save you."

Before I could move, he conjured a chain that wrapped itself around me, pinning my arms at my sides. I took a deep breath, flexed my chest, and the chains snapped just in time, allowing me to neutralize a shot he'd fired at my head.

I glanced up, then danced to my right. He countered by circling left. "Give it up, Hoarfrost," I said. "Come with me peaceably so Santa can help you. Don't make me hurt you."

He leaned against a tree, laughing. "Jingle. You're a fool, even dumber than I remembered." His shrill, high-pitched giggles sent birds fleeing the fronds above us. He fell onto the ground, rolling around in glee. "Hurt me? He's worried about hurting me. Too funny."

Perfect. Taking his eyes off me was what I wanted, and his last mistake of the evening. I signaled and the webbing that Santa had prepared settled onto him. It looked like a fishnet, but wasn't. It was a special elf-net designed to neutralize his powers.

He flailed against it, but the flailing quickly subsided as he lost strength in direct proportion to how strongly he jerked at the cords. Soon he lay motionless, almost comatose.

My three assistants settled in beside me.

"Sorry, sir," Flake said. "It took awhile to wake Ice and Snow. We got here as fast as we could."

"It's okay," I said. "The plan worked. That's the key thing. Santa and I anticipated his watching me and picking up on Ice and Snow." I placed my hands on their shoulders. "Sorry to put you in his sights, but I needed him to think he had taken out my team. Hope he didn't hurt you."

Ice rubbed his jaw. "I'll be okay. He packs a pretty good punch though."

"Yeah," Snow said. "Another week off will give me a chance to recover."

"In your dreams," I said. "But you can finish the vacation I interrupted. Be back Monday."

All four us laughed, not so much in mirth, but more in relief. I stared at Hoarfrost. "He's harmless now. Let's get him home to Santa. Be careful of the webbing though. It can't tell the difference between elves. Use the handles."

* * *

Santa stroked his beard as he paced in front of Hoarfrost. We were in Santa's study, and Hoarfrost sat in an easy chair, securely bound in the magic webbing. "You stole from children. There is no forgiveness for that. Your prior behavior pales in comparison to this. I can find no good in you. Do you understand?"

Hoarfrost sneered. "Why should I care what you think? You're finished—or you will be as soon as I'm free. You can't keep me down. I'm stronger than you."

Santa's expression turned to sadness. "You leave me no choice. I must call a meeting of the Council."

Hoarfrost's face fell, his bluster gone. Perhaps for the first time, he realized he'd gone too far. The Council convened only in the most severe cases.

"You're finished as a Santa elf," Santa said. "There is no rehabilitation when you steal from children. And don't think you'll escape. The last time, I allowed you to convince me you'd

51

repented. I won't make that mistake again." He turned to me. "Jingle, ask Martha to bring in the book."

"I have it right here," she said from the doorway where she held a tray. "I thought you'd need it, and I made some hot chocolate. Poor Hoarfrost looks like he can use a lift."

Flake said, "Ma'am—"

I signaled him to be quiet. Mrs. Clause loved all creatures, good and bad. She befriended anyone or anything that came near her.

"And here are extra marshmallows for those who want them."

Santa winked at me. "Thank you, Martha. Hot chocolate is nice. Ice, Flake, Snow." He nodded to the tray. "Help yourself. As Jingle knows, sipping is easier than arguing with my wife." He turned toward Hoarfrost. "I'll loosen your hands so you can join us."

"Santa," Ice said, his hand going to his jaw, "he—"

"Not to worry. I removed all his powers. He's harmless now. And it might be the last homey touch he has before he's sentenced. Prosit." He raised his mug, then sat down. "If you gentlemen will excuse me, I have some research to do. Jingle, please take your assistants and Hoarfrost into the living room. I'll join you shortly, then we'll call a meeting in the auditorium. We have justice to administer."

* * *

"My friends, I called you here to perform a sad duty," Santa said when the colony had gathered. "I'm sure you remember Hoarfrost Rime. Some of you referred to him as the frosty one. Anyway, Jingle discovered that Hoarfrost has committed *the* unforgivable sin." He paused as murmuring flew through the crowd. When he had everyone's attention again, he said, "He stole from children."

There was a collective gasp from the audience. Each of the elves and reindeer shook their heads, not wanting to believe. This hadn't happened in Santa Land in . . . in . . . They looked at one another. No one could remember when it last happened.

Santa continued, "I've checked the book. As I expected, the punishment is the most severe we have—incarceration in the Ice Prison for life." He held up his hand. "Before someone reminds me that there are other offenses that carry a similar sentence, such as reindeer maiming, let me add that his special detail will be making snowflakes."

Quizzical murmuring rose in volume until Santa cleared his throat, a clear sign for quiet. He turned to Hoarfrost. "I decree every snowflake around the world must be different. You will make millions, billions, even gazillions, and any time you duplicate one, you will do it again—and keep doing it until each is different." He paused. "For as long as you live."

THE END

You've met Jingle Bell, one of Santa's favorite elves. Now, we move on to Joseph, Sue and Ray's favorite cattle-herding burro. Of course, he is their only cattle-herding burro, but that doesn't take away from how special he is. Read on and you'll see the proof of my words.

ONCE UPON A CHRISTMAS

"Heehaw." Bet that got your attention. I may have a human name, but I'm a burro, a much higher form of mammal. Just wanted you to know. Yeah, yeah, you're thinking, animals can't talk, much less write. Well, you're straight on the writing bit. These hooves don't fit a computer keyboard. I'm narrating while my loyal scribe captures it on hard drive.

They call me Joseph. Or that's the way it is here on the ranch southwest of Waco. Sue, that's the human female that helps run this place, gave me the name. She said I was a Christmas present from Ray so she wanted something special. I should argue? Nah. I'm easygoing. As long as the grass is high, and there's water nearby, I'm happy. Call me Joseph, and I'll come running.

I'm a cattle-herding burro, raised from a colt to take care of livestock in a pasture or on open range. With or without fences, I've never lost a cow. When we have more time, I'll tell you some cow-burro stories, but this one is about Christmas.

It started early in December, which is a good time for a Christmas adventure to begin. However, the beginning did not forecast its ending.

It was early morning, and the sun had barely started its ascent. I was grazing some tall grass that grew along the fence closest to Sue and Ray's house.

With a bellow that sounded worse than Horatio the Bull when he steps in a fire ant hill, Ray came charging out the front door. They call their place the Sugar Shack. Not sure why. They just do. He waved his shotgun around like a lunatic, screaming, "Sue says you gotta die."

Before I could utter a heehaw, he dropped onto his belly, ripped off a section of the siding that covers the crawl space under the house, and blasted away. A few of the pellets ricocheted off the underpinnings, but most of them tore through the opposite side of the house.

My first reaction was to run as fast as I could to the other end of the pasture—other end of the ranch if I could cross the fences. I spun, but out of the corner of my eye saw several of my cows huddling together, their faces filled with fear. I couldn't leave them. They were my responsibility.

"Heehaw," I brayed, hoping Ray would hear me and quit firing. No such luck so I rushed to the cattle and head-butted them to get them to move. Finally, they broke into a trot and headed away from the shots.

As I returned my attention to Ray, he rolled over, re-loaded the shotgun, flipped back onto his stomach, and began to fire again. "I can't take it anymore," he yelled. "She's after me every minute."

Blam.

"Won't leave me alone."

Blam.

"Said either you leave or she leaves."

Blam.

Pause. He appeared to be thinking.

In a quieter voice, he said, "Maybe I should consider which might give me more peace." Silence. "Ah heck, she's a good cook."

Blam.

Only the fact I have large ears enabled me to hear his last remarks. He appeared to be talking to himself, not to his target—or anyone else. Don't make any cracks about my ears. They serve me well, and I'm proud of them.

"Sure hope Stinky's low in the hole," I heard. I looked around and standing in a large clump of grass was Mama Skunk and two of her kits.

"You live under the house?" I asked.

"Yes. Seemed like a good idea at the time. It's warm in the winter and cool in the summer." She turned to one of her young. "I told you not to encourage Stinky to test his glands."

I smiled. What else could I do? I remembered the time I surprised a mama skunk in her den with her little ones. It was an accident, but she didn't know it. She defended her home and family. Took days before anyone could stand the smell of me. I spent most of that time up to my eyeballs in the stock pond trying to wash the odor away. If Stinky had tested his power under the Sugar Shack, I understood Ray's behavior.

Mama Skunk looked at me, a tear trickling from her black eyes. "Can you stop him? If Stinky sticks his head up, it'll get blown off."

I considered the situation. Ray was in the process of re-loading, ejecting empties and cramming in live rounds as fast as he could. It didn't look like something that would guarantee a long life if I intervened. Then I studied Mama Skunk. Her tears would have moved the most hardened animal—even a human.

"Okay. I'll see what I can do." I leaned on the fence as I'd seen Horatio, the bull do. For him, that's all it took, leaning. For me, it took a lot of pushing, but the fence laid down enough so I could step over. Once free, I rushed toward the house screaming, "Heehaw, heehaw," at the top of my lungs. I wanted to yell, "Quit the stupid shooting," but I knew Ray wouldn't understand me. You humans have such a blockage about animals talking.

He rolled over and stared at me. Any moment I expected to see the gun swing around, but I kept charging. His face shaped itself into a big question mark, and I hoped it would stay that way.

However, as I ran, expecting the shotgun at any moment, another ingredient jumped into the feedbag. Sue charged out of the house.

"Ray, what are you doing? How can I make curtains when you're out here blasting away with that shotgun? I can feel the pellets slapping off my feet through the floorboards."

Since Ray was on his back, he was at a disadvantage with Sue straddling him. "Honey, you said I had to get rid of the skunks."

"Not with a shotgun, you idiot. Get some traps."

"We tried that. All we caught were your cats."

I started back toward the pasture, hoping the fence would lean both ways. It was no place for a burro named Joseph. Unfortunately, my right front hoof hit a can and sent it banging off the broken-down bulldozer sitting in the front yard. I cringed, knowing Sue's hearing was almost as good as mine.

"Joseph, what are you doing out of the pasture?" She picked up a branch and ran in my direction.

I did the honorable thing for a burro. I retreated as fast as I could. I'm not sure whether the fence leaned or I jumped it, but I ended up in the pasture with wire between Sue and me—a much safer situation.

"You'd better stay in there," she yelled as I made for a better position—the far side of the pasture. Once there, I pretended to be unaffected, nibbling the rich Texas grass. But out of the corner of my left eye, I watched the drama play out between Sue and Ray. It ended with him picking up his shell casings, emptying the shotgun, and re-entering the house. All the while, Sue chewed on his ear, explaining in no uncertain terms that shooting a twelve gauge under the Sugar Shack was not her idea of brilliance.

* * *

I didn't see Sue, Ray, or Mama Skunk and her little ones for the rest of the week. That may have been because I kept the herd as far from the Sugar Shack as I could. I was familiar with Sue's temper. Not something a simple burro needs to get next to. I also knew she was a really nice person and would, sooner or later, realize I hadn't done anything wrong. She owed me an apology, and I knew it would be forthcoming.

As expected, about a week later, Sue was at the fence calling me over.

"Joseph, want some sugar?" she said with more dripping from her lips than in her hand.

I eyed her without moving. As far as I was concerned at that moment, she was as attractive as an angry swarm of hornets.

"C'mon, Joseph. You can trust me. I know I was wrong. I have a surprise for you."

A human surprise? Didn't sound like something a burro should anticipate. I took a few tentative steps toward the fence.

"Remember the shotgun," a voice said.

I looked down and saw Mama Skunk eyeing Sue. She, Mama Skunk I mean, was careful to stay hidden in a tall patch of weeds.

"What's she got behind her back?" she asked.

When I returned my attention to Sue, I saw that her right hand held out the sugar cubes, but her left was out of sight.

"See what I mean?" Mama Skunk whispered.

"Yes." I stepped away from the fence and turned slightly, ready to bolt for the farthest reaches of the pasture if Sue made a suspicious move.

Salomi, a beautiful Arabian mare and the love of my life, pushed past me and ambled up to Sue as if there were no threats in the entire world.

Sue's hand began its move from behind her back, and I prepared to throw myself between my darling and the shotgun.

"Hello, Salomi," Sue said. "I brought you some, too." She held out her left hand, filled with sugar cubes.

Salomi whinnied softly and nuzzled Sue's hand, pulling the cubes in with her gorgeous lips.

"Joseph, if you don't take these, I'll give them to Salomi," Sue said, sticking her hand out toward me.

That did it. My fear vanished and I was soon sucking on the sweet treat. While I wasn't paying attention, Sue slipped a loop around my neck.

"Now, we'll go to the house, and get you cleaned up. I'm going to curry you until your coat shines."

My first impulse was to run, but that disappeared with her next words.

"I have some oats for you and after you've eaten, there may be more sugar. What do you think of that?" She slipped a rope around Salomi's neck. "Don't think I'd forget you, ol' girl. This is for both of you."

She led us to the gate, through it, and to the Sugar Shack. Ray waited with two buckets of soapy water. They worked on us, giving us scrubbings like never before. Sue gave me her full attention while Ray took Salomi. I suppose my height figured into it—only nine hands—and Sue is shorter than Ray. And, as you may have guessed, my lovely Salomi is much taller than I.

When Sue first started with the currycomb, it felt good, and I almost fell asleep under her gentle stroke. But she seemed to grow stronger with each touch and soon, the thought of escape entered my mind.

After an hour, I was ready to run to save my hide—literally—when Sue declared me ready. Ready for what? I wondered, but kept my thoughts to myself. With Ray and Salomi leading the way, Sue and I headed toward the horse trailer.

They loaded us, and I found myself staring at the wall, a window above my head. Salomi was in the next stall. I envied her. She could see through her window. It only took another moment and we were underway. Where, I had no idea.

I whispered to Salomi, "What's going on? Why are they acting so strange? I haven't been this clean since—" A revelation struck me. "Oh no, they're taking us to auction."

"What?" Salomi said. "But . . . yes, it could be. My last owner gave me a thorough cleaning before he sold me." She nuzzled my neck. "I'll miss you."

"That's all you have to say? You'll miss me? Well, I won't accept it. I simply will not. You know how I feel."

She opened her mouth, but before she spoke, the trailer came to a bumpy halt. A moment later, the tailgate dropped and Ray and Sue led us out.

The brightness of the sun made me squint, a disadvantage of big eyes. Sue walked toward a small group of people hovering around a fire in a barrel, pulling me along behind her. I could hear Ray and Salomi following.

"Here we are," Sue said. "This is Joseph, and the mare is Salomi. What do you think?"

The group split and walked around us, a couple of them stroking my flanks. One had the audacity to examine my teeth. I would have bitten him except I saw Sue giving me that look that said I'd pay if I misbehaved.

Salomi was less patient than I. She stamped her feet when a woman in a hideous hat said, "She has knots in her tail. Don't you ever brush her?"

Sue shot Ray a look that could broil cactus, but said nothing. I suspected he'd hear about it on the drive home. She was not one to let things go without comment.

The people finished their inspections, then walked back to the fire. Sue and Ray tied Salomi and me to the trailer and joined them. There was a lot of mumbling, head turning, and an occasional point in our direction.

I looked at Salomi. "Hope the same person buys both of us. See anyone that looks like a good owner?"

"They're humans," she said, then grinned. "They all look alike to me."

That's my honey. Delightful sense of humor.

She bent and mooched a mouthful of grass. "As long as the food is plentiful," she said while chewing, "I can live with it."

She seemed resigned to our separation, and that bothered me. Like her, I could live anywhere, but the thought of losing Salomi saddened me.

Sue walked toward us muttering under her breath. "Palomino. What a bunch of licorice jelly beans. Nowhere near the beauty of an Arabian like Salomi?"

She stopped between us and rubbed our noses. "Sorry, Salomi, they decided to go with Mr. Brannon's gelding. They'll rue that decision on Christmas Eve. But the good news is they think you're perfect, Joseph."

My heart tumbled to the bottom of my hooves. Her words sounded like I'd be moving on. I looked at Sue hoping the sadness in my eyes would cause her to change her mind. Then I nuzzled her.

"Lift your head," she said. "Lift your head and be proud. They considered five others, but chose you. That's quite an honor."

Not the way I saw it. As far as I was concerned, they could have the others. I wanted to stay with Salomi.

* * *

The next few days were busy—or as busy as Sue could keep me. You'd have thought she was preening me for a human beauty contest the way she worked on me. After she washed, brushed, and curried, she'd grab the scissors and trim what she called *wild hairs*. Believe me, with those blades flying around my eyes, ears, and other parts I hold dear, I stood especially still, barely breathing.

After declaring me beautiful, she'd lead me to a spot, then walk away after admonishing me not to move. I stood there, wondering why she was behaving in such a weird way, but knowing it couldn't last long. By her own words, Christmas Eve would soon arrive.

Depression filled every pore of my body. Salomi tried to raise my spirits, and Sue kept telling me how lucky I was, but I couldn't help but feel like the winner in an unluckiest burro contest.

As strange as it may sound, the one who most lifted my spirits was Mama Skunk. She was still determined to make her home under the Sugar Shack, and Ray just as determined to move her out. She told stories about the traps he set, and how Stinky raided them, stealing the bait before tripping them. When she described Ray's outrage, I'd crack up, my heehawing echoing throughout the herd. Especially, when Ray's embarrassment drove him to grab the shotgun and blast away at the underpinnings of his house. After the first episode with Ray's scattergun, Mama Skunk dug her lair deep enough for it to serve as a bunker. The only way Ray could get pellets into it would be to crawl under, put the barrel in the hole, and pull the trigger. Even then, Mama Skunk and her family would be safe because she dug in several twists and turns leading to the den.

A week passed—seven of the fastest days of my life. By my calculations, I had only four, maybe five, days left. I vowed to spend as much of it as possible with Salomi, but couldn't ignore the herd. As long as I was on the ranch, I had an obligation to do my job to the best of my abilities. The cattle would not suffer because of Ray and Sue's abysmal decision.

* * *

It was late afternoon when Sue came out of the Sugar Shack and walked to the fence. "Joseph, come over here. It's December twentieth, time for us to go into town."

61

The twentieth? I thought I had until Christmas Eve. I might be a burro, but I know when Santa visits.

I turned to run, but she said, "Don't make me come after you. You know I'll get you, and you'll be sorry."

I stopped, knowing she was right. There was no place to hide. I went to Salomi. "Guess this is it. I'll love you forever."

"You've been a wonderful friend," she said. "I'll never forget you. And I'll take care of the herd, not as good as you, but I'll give it my best." A tear trickled from her large brown eyes.

I sniffled and turned away, not wanting her to hear the sob that rattled in my chest.

"Let's go," Sue called. "I need to clean you up before we leave. I don't have all day."

After another thorough scrubbing and hard currying, she loaded me into the trailer. I was almost glad the day had arrived. My skin was tender from all the attention my coat had received. It would be nice to lie down and roll in the dust without Sue yelling at me.

Soon, Sue stopped at the place we'd visited with Salomi and Ray. Most of the same people were there, plus a few new faces. My guess was it would be an auction. I didn't care who would be my new master or mistress, I simply wanted it over.

I looked around, studying the grounds, the building, anything except the people. Maybe they'd think I was shy and not bid on me. I considered faking a limp, but figured Sue would make sure I didn't get away with it.

The structure was strange, not at all like the Sugar Shack. It had two wide doors and rose to a peak with a pole sticking up from the top. Instead of being clear, the windows had colored pictures in them. I held my head back and looked up. There was a cross at the tip of the spire. I knew what it was because Sue once showed me the one she wore and told me about it. She said it was a symbol of her religion, of someone named Jesus Christ who died for her.

Sue whispered in my ear, "Stand up, Joseph. Don't slouch when you're at church."

Okay, that answered one question. But why hold an auction at a place of worship?

The crowd parted as we neared, and behind them, I saw another building—smaller, but stranger. It looked like a stable except it was open across the front. Inside were the normal things we find in a stable—straw on the floor, stalls for livestock, a trough for feed, a water barrel—sparse for humans, perfect for animals. We don't need fancy gewgaws to make us happy.

A woman in a strange dress stepped forward. Now Sue wears some funny-looking stuff when she's bush-hogging the fields, but this lady's was stranger. It looked like a colorful sheet draped around her with a matching pillow case over her head.

"Oh Sue," she gushed, "he's perfect."

A man I hadn't seen before, in some kind of colorful robe, said, "He don't bite, does he? A jackass bit me once."

Ha. If he had called him a jackass, no wonder he took a hunk out of him. Burros are a proud lot, and that pride says we're not jackasses. Donkey, yes. Jackass, no.

"Now, Simon," Sue said, "you know I wouldn't have a dangerous animal around."

"Uh-huh," Simon said. "How 'bout that dang cat of yourn that attacked me last year?"

"Wasn't his fault. You came straight from the fishing hole and smelled like catfish. Albatross thought you'd taste the same."

The woman laughed. "I can vouch for the way you smell sometimes, but I don't find it appetizing. Only a cat could love you."

"That's pretty catty, Lauren," he said, grinning. "Besides, it don't change the fact Sue's danged animal attacked me."

"Joseph's different," Sue said. "He's as docile as a pussycat, uh, I mean . . ." She chuckled. "Joseph's not at all like Albatross. He doesn't like fish." She threw her hand over her mouth as laughter bubbled out in an unladylike fashion.

Lauren said, "This is fun, but let's see if it'll work. We have four nights to get the kinks out, to make sure the whole town doesn't watch us stumble all over one another."

If you're confused, you know how I felt. I came expecting an auction, and this Lauren person was talking nonsense. Any fool could see I was a great buy, and it wouldn't take any four nights for it. I decided to heck with them. If they wanted to play, they could pay. I lifted my head and strutted past Lauren like I owned the place. The stable-like structure appeared to be the center of activity so I headed in that direction.

"Hold on, Joseph," Sue said, pulling on my halter. "Don't rush it. We start offstage."

* * *

I'm not often wrong, but that time I may have set a new world record. On Christmas Eve, Simon led me into the churchyard with Lauren on my back. I took small steps to slow the trip as a large group of townspeople watched. We headed straight for the phony stable where Lauren dismounted and, with great difficulty, waited beside me, a gentle touch on my reins.

Simon pretended to talk to a man—the innkeeper they called him—then returned to us. "Mary, my dear, they have no rooms, and there are none in town. They only have one stable empty. The straw is clean." He waved his arm in a theatrical gesture. "We can stay here."

Lauren overacted, rolling her eyes, and said, "Yes. I am so tired. We must stop. Our son will be born here."

The lights dimmed, and we scurried to new positions. When they brightened again in a few minutes, I was ground hitched, and the palomino, two sheep, a dog, and a cat had joined us. Several other humans were present—some dressed as what they called shepherds and three as wise men.

But most important, a baby lay in the straw-filled manger. He gurgled as if born to be there. Lauren and Simon knelt beside him as soft background music lent to the atmosphere.

Away in a manger, no crib for a bed,
The little Lord Jesus laid down his sweet head.

While I didn't understand all that was happening, I could see the love in the eyes of the spectators and the pride on the faces of Lauren and Simon.

I'm not sure what came over me, but suddenly, I felt twenty hands tall. Everyone was watching, and I loved it. Arching my neck, I let out the loudest heehaw I've ever sung.

It was my best Christmas ever.

THE END

AUTHOR COMMENT: Yep, Joseph is a special burro. But Sue, Ray, and I aren't the only ones who think that. Read on and you'll discover another of his admirers.

A STORMY CHRISTMAS EVE

There are evenings when the sky is so bright and the stars so low, I feel like if I stretch my neck a little extra, I can graze on them. I've often wondered how they would taste—thorny like a cactus leaf or sweet like the petals of a daisy. Such was the ceiling I stood under early on Christmas Eve.

Soft music floated through the air from the party hosted by Sue and Ray. Christmas carols played in the Sugar Shack. One of my favorites was in progress.

Long time ago in Bethlehem,
So the Holy Bible say.
Mary's Boy Child, Jesus Christ,
Was born on Christmas Day.

It was special because I'd had the privilege the previous year to be part of a nativity scene, the important role of carrying Mary to the manger where the baby Jesus would be born. Definitely a high point in my life.

Sorry. You're probably confused. I'll explain. My name is Joseph, and I'm a cattle-herding burro. There aren't many of us around, but the few I've met are proud of the occupation. I take care of a small herd for Sue and Ray, humans who own a ranch southwest of Waco. They are both nice, although, of the two, Sue has the hotter temper. She's quick to grab a switch and swat my backside if I don't meet her expectations.

They moved here a few years ago, seeking peace in retirement. After buying the ranch, they lived in a travel trailer while building the Sugar Shack. That's what Sue calls their house. They built it themselves. I know because I watched, not believing it. The other ranch houses I've seen go up were built by a gang of men. I guess Ray and Sue didn't know that. The only time they brought in extra hands was when something was too heavy for the two of them to handle—and that wasn't often.

Anyway, while their new home was under construction, Ray began to stock the ranch. He attended auctions and bought cattle and Horatio the bull to get things going. Then he purchased me as a Christmas gift for Sue their first year here. She promptly dubbed me Joseph because of the season.

Ray enjoys auctions. I've heard him mumble it gets him away from Sue and her chores. Anyway, one day he came home with Salomi, a beautiful, black Arabian mare. Wow. It was love at first sight—well, on my side anyway. She was gorgeous.

Ray said any self-respecting ranch had to have horses. He wanted others so he and Sue could ride the range. Sue's response left no doubt that one horse was enough. Ray just grinned. I guess he's heard her blow long enough to know when she was serious versus when there's a big storm coming. To me, when she's wound up, she's pretty frightening all the time. But he didn't bring any other horses home from auction.

The song changed to a lively version of *Santa Claus is Coming to Town*, making me study the horizon. Dark clouds loomed, a cold front moving in. I hoped it wouldn't bring foul weather although that would help me. You see, I was concerned about cow-tippers, and a cold rain might keep them away. But Santa was out there somewhere, and I didn't want anything slowing him down. The children waited.

Like I said, I was alert for cow-tippers. For those of you from New York City who've never heard of it, let me explain. The theory is you can slip up on a snoozing cow and push her over. It's almost a myth because most cows are light sleepers. Approach as quiet as a mole in his burrow, and they'll awaken. And you can't tip an alert cow.

Note that I said most cows. I have one of the hardest sleeping cows on the planet in my herd. Her name is Ethel. Not much danger of anyone catching Z's when she's zonked. The snores speak thick volumes. For that reason, the rest of the herd race away as soon as she closes her eyes.

The first time someone tipped her was last Halloween. The way I figured it, three teens sneaked up on Ethel, two on one side and one on the other. The one began to push. She woke and leaned into him to keep from falling over. He dropped back and the other two shoved from the opposite side. Over she went—plop.

Her tumble and their laughter woke me as they raced from the pasture with Ethel hot on their heels. When she saw me, she slid to a halt and yelled at me. For days, she dogged me, never letting up. She wouldn't close her eyes until I promised to stay by her side. Needless to say, I didn't get much sleep. I folded my ears down, but her snores still got through.

The cow-tippers next attack came on Thanksgiving. That time they went after Samantha, but she woke up before they could do their deed. However, I now had both Ethel and Samantha demanding a bodyguard every night. And, Samantha refused to be anywhere near Ethel because of the snoring. What's a burro to do? I did the best I could. I stationed myself halfway between them and kept my eyes open. Two weeks passed before we relaxed. Two sleepless weeks for me.

Then several days ago, while I grazed the fence along the road, a group of the neighborhood teenagers walked by making plans for Christmas Eve. Usually, it was some trickery regarding Santa. You know, the usual kid stuff—swiping his sled while he was in a house, hobbling one of his reindeer, grabbing packages, and other equally dumb ideas doomed to failure. I probably don't need to tell you that Santa left them more chunks of coal than presents.

That day's conversation was different though.

"What we gonna do to Santa Christmas Eve?" the smallest kid said. Everyone called him Shorty.

"We're too old for that," Dan, their leader, said. "We need something different, something that'll make us legends in school."

"Yeah, what's that?"

"I'm thinking. Don't rush me."

They walked in silence for several yards, then Dan said, "We need a trick that's never been done before. Something big. Something folks'll remember."

"This ain't exactly Waco out here," Shorty said. "There ain't nothing here that's *big*. Nothing but cows and horses and pastures."

"Oh, shut up and let Dan think," a third kid said. "Your whining's enough to put the cows to sleep."

Dan stopped and punched the last speaker on the arm. "That's it. Tommy, you're good, real good."

"Huh?" Tommy said, rubbing his bicep. "Wha'd I say?"

"Put the cows to sleep. That's what we're gonna do. Well, not exactly. We're gonna give them a wakeup that everybody'll remember for years."

If it appears I don't have much respect for the intelligence of humans, there's one example why. The kids made their plans right in front of me. They actually walked over and sat alongside the road, close to the fence where I pretended to graze. Their idea was to gather all their friends, hit one herd, and tip as many cows as they could. After listing the kids, Dan said they could easily get twenty cows—a new Texas record.

It was about all I could do to keep from laughing. I kept my muzzle in the tall grass so none of them would see the big grin I wore. But the next part made me want to jerk my head up.

Shorty said, "What herd we gonna hit? My pa'll skin me alive if we go near ours."

"Same here," Tommy said. "Ain't no way I'm going along if you mess with my pappy's cows. He'd ground me 'til I'm thirty-seven."

Similar comments came from each of the teens, including Dan. They sat with their chins resting in their hands, the very picture of stumped.

I was afraid I would run out of grass before they finished planning. As it was, I cleared about fifteen feet before Dan said, "My daddy always says, when you have a problem, break it down into little pieces. Then, solve each one and soon, you'll have the solution to all."

"Big deal," Shorty said. "What's the little parts?"

"First, we need a small herd. No need going where there's hundreds when we only have a few guys. Where do we find a small herd in this area?"

He looked into my pasture.

Uh-oh, I thought.

"Second, we need a herd that doesn't belong to any of us. That way, our daddies will just laugh when we tell 'em what we done. Where do we find a small herd that doesn't belong to the parents of any of the gang?"

Each of them looked into my pasture.

Uh-uh-oh, I thought.

"Last, we need a herd that ain't got no protection, no dog that'll go barking his head off. Where can we find a herd like that?"

Their heads turned as one toward my cattle.

Oh no, I thought.

"Yeah," Shorty said. "All they got is that broken-down jackass."

They bounced up and laughed as they walked away, slapping one another on the back.

I followed as far as I could, but all I heard was what I already knew. They were going to get the gang together and hit my herd hard on Christmas Eve. The crack about a jackass was just flowers in the weeds, adding sweetness to my stopping them.

After considering the situation, surveying the area, and putting my enormous mental powers to work, I came up with a plan. I called a meeting with Horatio and Salomi in the corner where the fences joined. Since I didn't want Sue or Ray to see us, I scheduled it during the evening.

"Horatio, will you come over into the cows' pasture Christmas Eve? I'd like you in the middle of the herd where no one can see you. If you wait until the sun has completely set, you can escape Sue's sharp eyes."

"Sure, little buddy. I'll lean on the fence and sneak in."

"Great. Salomi, will you take a position right here? Since you're taller, you can see over the herd and sound a warning. Just sing out with your lovely voice."

"Yes, Joseph," she said. "I'll do anything you say." Her left eye winked. I hoped it was on purpose.

"Good. That takes care of the herd and a lookout. I'll put myself in the center of the pasture where I can see all around." I stopped and thought. "That's the best plan I can come up with. The weakness is communication. We'll have to stay alert and react to the one who spots trouble first. Any comments?"

"I can help."

The three of us looked for the voice.

"Down here in the weeds. It's me."

It was Mama Skunk. If she hadn't had the white streaks down her back, I might not have seen her. "Hello," I said. "How can you help?"

"Stinky and I can carry messages. No one can see me when I streak through the tall grass."

"Sounds good to me," Horatio said. "You won't get stepped on, will you?"

"No. The cows are used to us being around their hooves."

"How about Stinky?" Salomi said. "Can we trust him to behave?"

"I wish you'd give him another chance," Mama Skunk said, a sad tone in her voice. "I know he sprayed you that time, but he swears he didn't know his glands had reloaded. He's changed, you know."

"Yeah. I believe every word of that," Salomi said. She left no doubt she meant the opposite.

"Stinky could stay with me," I said. "If he has an *accident*, I'll make sure he pays for it." I considered the setup. "Let's do it. Mama Skunk, you join Horatio and send Stinky to me. You'll have to cover Salomi, too, but that shouldn't be hard because I want the herd in the corner of the pasture."

Everyone agreed to the plan. I said, "Okay, let's all—"

"Can we do one more thing?" Mama Skunk asked.

"What is it," Salomi asked in an impatient voice. She rates skunks only a few notches above fire ants.

"After we do our communication jobs, can we go over to the fence near the road. Those boys throw rocks every time they see us. I'd like to plan a little surprise for them."

I studied her, then glanced at Horatio and Salomi. They looked like I felt. Through a grin, I said, "Go for it. Now, is that everything?"

All three nodded, so I adjourned the meeting. As they walked away, I considered the plan and smiled. Horatio's bellow would scare those kids right out of their stocking caps. And they wouldn't know he was there until it was too late for them to make a quick escape. We'd be as far from the road as possible. With five sets of eyes peeled for the invaders, we should be ready.

Some of the heifers argued with me—they didn't want to be anywhere near Ethel's snores—but I finally won them over. Ethel agreed to stay awake until I gave the all-clear, but I didn't put much credence in her words. She could drop off in the middle of chewing her cud. I placed myself in the middle of the pasture where I could see in all directions.

That's why I was apprehensive on Christmas Eve, worried what a storm would do to Santa, but hoping one would roll in soon enough to discourage the cow-tippers. My plan was solid, considering what I had to work with, but if ten or twenty kids hit us, there was only so much we could do. They might not tip any cows, but they could scare them. My job was to ensure nothing happened.

* * *

I checked the horizon again. The dark clouds raced forward, now covering almost half the sky. The stars were disappearing at an alarming rate. Soon, it would be pitch black, making it all but impossible to see across the pasture. If the rain came, I could relax, but if it didn't . . .

"You see that?"

I looked down, knowing Stinky was nearby. He stood by my rear legs, staring toward the road.

"There's humans out there," he said. "They're skulking along the fence line."

I peered into the darkness. "Are you sure? I don't see anything."

"You're too tall. From down here, I can see them against the sky. You're looking at them against the tree line."

I glanced in the direction of the herd, hoping to spot Horatio. Yes, there he was. I next checked for Salomi, but couldn't see her. Her beautiful, black coat blended into the darkness.

There. Movement along the fence. The humans were moving faster, and that helped me see them.

"Okay, I have them," I said. "You know what to do. Take off."

"No problem." He disappeared in the tall grass, leaving nothing more than swaying stalks to mark his passage.

A few minutes later, he was back. "Horatio is ready. I swung by and told Salomi, too." He hesitated. "Can I go now? I want to catch up with Mama. I need to help her. She's pretty upset with those rock-throwers."

"Sure." I grinned. "Get your revenge."

Once more, he disappeared without a sound.

I checked the teens' progress. Just a few more minutes, and my trap would spring. Looking toward the herd, I saw the cows shifting position, opening a path for Horatio. That brought a smile to my muzzle as I pictured the flight of the would-be cow-tippers.

The clouds were overhead now, leaving only an uncovered horizon where the stars continued to twinkle. The moon hung trapped above the blackness.

A horrendous roar caused me to jump ten feet straight up. Okay, maybe not ten feet, but higher than I'd ever jumped before. A pounding of hooves accompanied the noise as Horatio stormed through the lane in the herd. A split second later, Salomi let out a neigh that echoed across the land, and my heehaw joined them as I merged with Horatio's charge.

You've probably heard the expression, *running like a scared rabbit*. Well, those kids outran any rabbit in the state, scared or otherwise. They tore across the pasture like the devil himself was on their heels. The faster ones reached the fence and vaulted it. As they landed, they let out a scream of anguish, gagging as they stumbled into the ditch filled with six-day-old rainwater—stagnant and slimy.

The slower ones ran into the fence and fell backwards. Then they crawled over or under the fence and followed their friends.

Shorty was last in line. By then, Mama Skunk and Stinky's spraying must have created a cloud of skunk musk at its thickest.

He tried to climb over, but his foot caught the top rail, and he splattered face forward into the ditch. Perfect justice for his crack about jackasses. I won't quote what he said when he came up with rotting weeds hanging from his face. Not an appetizing sight—even for a burro.

Horatio and I skidded to a halt at the fence, then backtracked several yards before stopping. There was no doubt Mama Skunk and Stinky had been there. A dunking in the stock tank was in order for both of us. Meanwhile, the teenagers disappeared into the darkness.

"That should keep them away for a while," Horatio said.

As soon as I quit chortling, I agreed with him, then we headed for the herd who were on their knees, locked in laughter.

Halfway there, I said, "Did you hear that?"

"Hear what? All I hear is Ethel giggling louder than she snores, and that's too loud for me." He broke into a trot toward his pasture. "I'm going home and get some rest. It stinks over here. If you need me, give a heehaw."

I started to call thank you, but stopped when I heard the sound again. It was bells—the tinkling of small bells, and it came from above. I looked up, but saw only black clouds rolling and boiling as a storm pushed them forward.

I shuddered, expecting a cold rain soon. Not that I couldn't handle it. After all, I wear a waterproof coat, but it would make for a long night. I hoped there would be no thunder and lightning. It wouldn't bother me, but my herd might panic with the first crash. In past storms, I had my hands full keeping them from banging into the fences. And hail. That stuff hurt, plus the racket it makes slamming into the roof of the Sugar Shack. It only puts the cattle in a more frightful mood.

The bells again. The sound seemed to be coming from the north, but I couldn't be sure because the wind had picked up and was now keening past my ears. There was another sound. Laughter? Ho, ho, ho? I stared into the clouds, willing them to open and show me the source of the tinkling. And they did. Well, not quite, but a team of reindeer appeared, followed by a sleigh. Santa?

I watched with wide eyes as he settled the team beside me. In all my years of patrolling on Christmas Eve, such had never happened. I wanted to step up and welcome him, but couldn't move. I couldn't speak. I was aghast. Santa had landed beside me.

"Hello, Joseph," he said, just like we were old friends.

"You, you know me?" I stuttered.

"Ho, ho, ho. Of course. I know all creatures, big and small, human and otherwise. That's my job, you know. Just like yours is to watch over your herd."

"Yes sir, of course, I mean, uh, uh . . ."

Santa let out a huge laugh, and sure enough, his belly shook like a bowlful of jelly. "Relax, Joseph. I had to set down here. I need some help, perhaps from you."

"Yes sir, of course, I mean, uh, uh, uh . . ."

He stepped out of the sleigh, laid his hand on my flank, then gently stoked my coat. "If you don't settle down, you'll never be able to assist me. And if you can't, I fear many children will be disappointed when the sun comes up. Now get ahold of yourself."

"I can, I will," I said. And I did. It wasn't easy, but I squared my shoulders and lifted my head. "What do you need?"

"Cupid hurt his ankle on the roof of your neighbor's house." He grimaced. "Life was simpler before satellite dishes, especially those little ones. They're so hard to see when it storms. Anyway, I need to send him home. But that will leave me a team member short, and there's still a long night in front of us. Without him, I might not make my schedule, but if I keep him in harness . . ."

I stared at the reindeer and spotted Cupid. He wore a stoic expression while holding his right front leg in the air. Even in the darkness, I could see it was larger than the left. "What can I do?" I glanced at my herd. They were quiet. "I don't want the children disappointed."

Santa gave me a strange look. "Have you ever flown? Do you get airsick?"

I glanced over both shoulders, wondering if someone else had walked up, maybe a fairy or something. "Me? You talking to me?"

Santa's belly shook again. "Of course. Why do you think I landed here? You're about the same size as Cupid. I bet his harness will fit you—if you're willing."

"But I can't fly, and if you walk, you'll never get to all the children. I don't understand."

Santa laughed again. "Stand beside Cupid, and let's see if the harness fits. That's the first problem."

What would you have done? I did the same. I walked over and stood shoulder to shoulder with Cupid. As Santa said, we were about the same height. Funny, I'd always assumed reindeer were much bigger. I mean, that's a heavy sleigh they pull.

"Wonderful. You're the right size," Santa said. "It's my lucky day."

"But—"

"Only question left is, are you willing to help us?"

"Of course, but—"

"Save your butts for Ethel when she snores too loud." He stopped and stared at me. "Butts, like head butts.? Get it?"

His reindeer groaned.

"All right, you guys." He turned back to me. "What is it you're trying to say?"

"I can't fly."

"Hmmm, yes, that would be a problem if I weren't Santa. Christmas Eve is the most magical night of the year." He turned to Cupid. "Slip out of your harness and help me get Joseph into it."

One of the reindeer snorted and stamped a foot.

"Blitzen, why are you so impatient? For years, I've been trying to teach you patience. Everything will be all right. We'll only be a few more minutes."

He turned his attention to me. "Joseph, stand still and let us strap you in."

I did as told and soon stood in line where Cupid had been. I had no clue what I was supposed to do. I'd never been part of a team before.

"Cupid," Santa said. "Fly home and tell Rudolph to rendezvous with us. Then take care of that ankle. Stick it in a snow bank for a couple of hours to keep the swelling down. I'll have Martha make up a hot soak tomorrow, and you can treat it while the rest of the team and I catch up on our sleep. Oh, tell Martha everything is fine. Joseph is flying with us until Rudolph finds us."

"Huh," I said, the situation becoming real. "I'm going to . . . to fly?"

"You said you'd help."

"I know, but—"

"Take off, Cupid. Everything is under control."

Cupid rose into the air and with a last look, flew northward.

"Okay, Joseph. Let's get out of here. Maybe we can get in front of this weather. My furs are good, but I still hate stormy nights."

"Uh, Santa. Did you forget—"

"Oh my. Martha says I'm getting absentminded. Guess she's right." He laid his palm on my forehead and stroked down between my eyes. Then he walked around me, running his hands down each leg.

The most amazing feeling came over me. I felt so light, like I was floating, but when I looked down, my feet were still on the ground. And strong—as strong as a bull, even as strong as Horatio, who was stronger than any bull I'd ever met. I knew I could fly, and I knew I could pull that sleigh.

"Ready, Joseph?" Santa asked.

"Oh, yes sir," I answered. "I'm ready, willing, and anxious to get off the ground. Can we go?"

Santa let out another guffaw. "Of course. When Rudolph catches up, I'll send you home. Don't worry about getting lost. I put the flight plan in your head." He climbed into the sleigh. "Okay, everybody ready? Let's do it. Ho, ho, ho."

From the Sugar Shack, I heard

> *Here comes Santa Claus,*
> *Here comes Santa Claus,*
> *Right down Santa Claus lane.*

Santa drowned it out by calling, "Go Dasher, Dancer, Prancer, and Vixen. Up Comet, Cu—whoops, Joseph—Donner and Blitzen. To the top of the trees, above every moo, now fly away, fly away, we have work to do."

We rose into the air with the sleigh following. I felt normal, like I'd done this forever. "Heehaw," I brayed into the night. The storm opened up, but I didn't care. I was flying with Santa and his reindeer. Behind me, I heard Santa's ho, ho, ho and pictured the jiggling belly covered by his red suit.

It was a night I'll never forget. And maybe you remember it, too. Was there a Christmas Eve when you thought you might have heard a burro braying above you? It might not have been the eggnog.

THE END

79

AUTHOR COMMENT: So Joseph was given magical powers and allowed to fly Santa's sleigh with the other reindeer. I can understand his excitement. Now, on to another adventure without Santa's intervention.

Joseph and Noel

It was morning, December 24th, Christmas Eve. For a reason I couldn't identify, I sensed something big coming my way, something bigger than just Christmas. I stood near the south fence, munching on tender grass. The herd was scattered behind me, each of them enjoying the winter growth. One of the great things about winter was no fire ants, so I didn't have to worry about one of my group sticking a muzzle into a fire ant mound. I don't know where the ants go, but I'm always happy to wave bye-bye. Of course, they don't bother to say farewell, they just disappear. Even as I surveyed the area to make sure everything was fine, that feeling of something big happening stayed with me.

Oh, my. Here I go again, forgetting to introduce myself. I'm not really so conceited I expect everyone to know me, but sometimes I forget. My name is Joseph. I'm a cattle-herding burro on a small ranch southwest of Waco. My owners are Sue and Ray. They're from back east somewhere so I've had my hooves full teaching them the business. We've been at it about four years, and I'm proud to say they've come along nicely. They started with a small herd of cattle, a bull, an Arabian mare, and me. The herd has almost doubled while the rest of us have stayed the same.

Salomi, the Arabian mare, stood beside me munching breakfast as I was. She lifted her head and said, "Uh-oh. Somebody's gonna get a bath."

I looked up and saw Sue marching our way. She carried a halter in one hand and a bucket in the other. "You're right. Or maybe both of us." I figured what will be, will be, and went back to my munching, but kept one eye on Sue.

"Joseph. Come over here." It was Sue at the gate. Apparently, I was her *lucky* choice.

Salomi nuzzled me. "Time to face the music. Don't come back smelling too sweet or Hazel will never let you live it down."

I groaned and trotted toward Sue.

For the next hour or so, I was put through a Sue ritual—a thorough washing, then currying until my skin was tender. She brushed at my tail so long I could only hope there was a hair left. And my mane. Well, when she started, I had a short mane. When she finished, I felt the need to check my reflection in the stock tank to see if I had anything.

I wanted to ask her why, but humans aren't multilingual like animals so I'd have been wasting my time.

Finally, she said, "That's it, Joseph. I have big plans for you tomorrow, and you need to look your best. That's Christmas Day, you know. So, stay clean, or I'll get a switch. Right now, I have to get back to the Sugar Shack before Ray messes up the tree. We have people coming over this evening for eggnog and cookies. I want the tree to be perfect. Every year, he covers up the lights with the tinsel. I have to uncover them and supervise him putting the angel on top. Remember what I said." She walked me to the gate and turned me into the pasture.

I wanted to ask her what she meant, but, of course, I couldn't. Big plans for tomorrow? Oh, no. Was she selling me down the road? She'd threatened to do it many times when I did something she considered wrong. Of course, she had usually jumped to an incorrect conclusion. Another of the times when being able to talk to her would have come in handy. But, since I couldn't converse with her, I'd take off running. Her switches stung.

I trotted to where Salomi stood with Horatio. "I'm back. Wasn't too bad."

"Oh, don't you smell nice?" Horatio said. "Ain't that a nice aroma, Salomi?"

"Oh, yes," she said. "Should we call Hazel over so she can have a sniff?"

"Don't you dare," I said. "You know she'll raze me from here to roundup."

Both laughed as Star came running up. "Uncle Joseph, where have you been? I missed you."

Star was Hazel's calf, the first born in the herd. I had the pleasure of naming her to match the white star on her forehead. Since Hazel was not a good mother, I spent a lot of Star's early days watching out for her—and that was a chore. She got into about every kind of mischief I've ever seen and a couple I'd never encountered before. Anyway, that led her to call me Uncle.

"I was at—"

"What's that funny smell?" she said. "It's kind of sweet, too sweet." She sniffed me. "Is that you? You're like an overripe cantaloupe. You better watch out. The honeybees will be after you."

"Just never you mind."

She laughed and started dancing around me, kicking up dust.

"I'd appreciate it if you wouldn't do that," I said. "I have to stay clean for tomorrow. Sue has plans for me. I think she's selling me down the road."

Star stopped, mid-step. "No. She can't do that. I won't let her."

"And how do you propose to stop her?" Salomi said. "We belong to Sue and Ray. They can do whatever they please."

"Well . . . well . . . I won't like it, not one little bit. I won't be nice to her anymore."

"Why are you standing here in this terrible stink? It reeks."

I looked around, trying to locate the voice, then realized I knew the source. I scanned the grass and saw Stinky staring up at me. "What do you mean stink? I smell nice."

Stinky was the youngest boy in the family of skunks who lived in the area. He was also the most mischievous, always on the edge of, or in the middle of, getting into trouble.

"Maybe to you, but to me, ugh. I'll get the family over here. If we work together, we can make you more agreeable."

"Don't you dare," I said. "And the rest of you, quit laughing. Sue wants it like this, and I'm not gonna change it."

Stinky ran off through the grass, his giggle hanging in the air behind him.

I couldn't take it anymore. I trotted off to a far corner of the pasture where I spent the rest of the day, ducking everyone. I didn't mean to be antisocial, but the ribbing was too much—especially for Christmas Eve.

* * *

That evening, Salomi and I stood by the fence closest to the Sugar Shack, listening to the snatches of conversation coming from the partiers. The humans appeared to be having a wonderful time. Then, the sound of Christmas carols took over. The Mormon Tabernacle Choir would not have been challenged, but even the clinkers sounded good to my tall burro ears.

> *Hark the herald angels sing*
> *"Glory to the newborn King!*
> *Peace on earth and mercy mild*
> *God and sinners reconciled"*

That was followed by

> *Jingle Bells, Jingle Bells.*
> *Jingle all the way.*
> *Oh, what fun it is to ride*
> *In a one-horse open sleigh.*

And many more. The singing went on for an hour or more, making me so happy I had been adopted by Sue and Ray. I leaned against Salomi and nuzzled her. Could life be better?

Gradually, the music died away, and the party came to a close. As the people streamed out to their cars and trucks, I turned away from the fence. To my surprise, I saw the whole herd and Horatio lined up behind me. I don't know when they arrived, but they appeared as happy and satisfied as I. Indeed, Christmas Eve was the most wonderful night of the year.

* * *

The next morning, Christmas, I woke early to a beautiful day.

83

The sky was cloudless, and the temperature was comfortable. Dew hung heavy on the grass, making it appear to glisten. The beauty added to my feelings of anticipation. Underlying it, however, was sadness as I considered a new life—if Sue sold me down the road. Try as hard as I could, I couldn't come up with another reason I was spruced up and Sue said she had *big plans* for me.

I had breakfast with Salomi, neither of us having much to say. We'd said it all Christmas Eve. Then, I wandered through the herd, wishing each of them a Merry Christmas. When I got to Star, it was a chore to hold back the tears that fought to escape.

Last, I went to Horatio and thanked him for all the help he'd given me during our time together. For a little guy like me, it was always good to have a big bruiser for a close friend. He'd been there for me several times, the most recent being when wild hogs tried to take over the pasture.

As I walked to the gate to wait, Stinky came running up. "Good luck, Joseph. Thank you for all your help."

I nodded to him then broke into a trot. It was either get off by myself or make a jackass of myself, bawling in front of everyone. Christmas Day should be a day of happiness, not a day to show sadness and weakness.

* * *

The sun was high overhead when Sue came out the front door, dressed in Christmas finery. Ray followed her and pulled the truck around to the back of the Sugar Shack. Sue waited, pacing back and forth, until he came back with the horse trailer hooked behind the pickup. She climbed in and they drove to the pasture gate.

When Sue got out, she had a harness in her hand. She walked over to me and rubbed the top of my head. It was something she often did when she felt good toward me. As she turned away, I realized the world smelled different. Within a few more minutes, I wore the harness and had been loaded into the horse trailer.

"You just relax," Sue said. "We have a trip to take. It's mostly paved so it won't be too bumpy."

I wanted to ask her where we were going, but, of course, I couldn't. She climbed out of the trailer, and I heard the door latch. Here we go, I thought. Down the road.

I am not fond of riding in the horse trailer. Salomi enjoyed it. She said she loved to watch the countryside fly by—all the pastures and houses and even the towns. It was a thrilling experience for her every time she went for a ride.

For me, it was different. It's not that it scares me or makes me sick, but I don't like being closed in, staring at a blank wall. The trailer had windows along the side, but they were at Salomi's height. Me, I was too short to see through them. No matter how I stretched my neck, I could only see wall. If I could speak human, I'd ask Ray to cut a window down at my height. But, that was another thing I couldn't do, so I was doomed to stare at the wall. If the ride was smooth enough, I could maybe take a nap, but I knew it wouldn't last long. The trailer would hit the inevitable bump, and I'd be jarred awake. After the first few rides, I gave up trying to sleep.

On this day, I spent my time thinking about Salomi, Horatio, Star, Hazel, Stinky, and the rest of the herd. It had been good years with them. I'd met the mare of my dreams and found a best friend. Also, I'd had the pleasure of watching Star grow from a newborn to the young heifer she was now. Even Hazel, who had given me the miseries so many times, rested in a soft spot in my heart. I wanted to laugh when I thought of Stinky. He was so full of energy and so full of mischief I didn't see how he could live a long life. However, one thing was for sure, while he was alive, he'd have fun. The herd—my responsibility. I'd done the best by them I knew how. Not one had been injured by coyotes, wolves, snakes, fire ants, or any of the other dangers that lurk in Texas. I was proud of that and hoped Sue and Ray would bring in a competent replacement for me. The herd was vulnerable to so many perils without a good protector.

As I reminisced, I realized the trailer was slowing. Must be there, I thought. Wherever there is. We veered to the right, followed by a bumpy slow-down, then a stop.

I heard Ray say, "You need some help? How can we help you?"

Another voice said, "Thank you for stopping, mister. Now, you can help us by getting out of the pickup—you and the woman. Don't make me use this thing."

"Huh? What's with the gun?" Ray said. "What are you doing?"

"You're pretty dumb, aren't you? We're taking your rig. We

need it more than you do."

"What? Not a chance. You can't do that." The voice was Ray's.

"This gun says I can. Hey, woman, get around here where I can keep an eye on you. What you got in the trailer?"

There was a period of silence, allowing me time to think. I'd heard about something called carjacking. Was this pickup-truck-and-horse-trailer-jacking? Sounded like it.

"I asked you a question, woman. What's in the trailer?"

Sue answered, "Nothing except our burro. We're taking him to—"

"Wrong. You *were* taking him. Now, you, your buddy, and the jackass are walking." This was followed by a laugh. "Rusty, get that jackass out of the trailer, then get ready to roll this rig out of here. I'll follow in our truck."

"Yo, Cactus. I got it."

You can probably guess how I felt about being called a jackass. I promised they'd pay for it. They'd better not relax a second.

Next, there was a fumbling at the door, then it swung open. I was ready to fight, but saw a scruffy-looking man standing there holding Sue by her arm. I couldn't risk her.

She climbed into the trailer and untied my halter. "Come with me, Joseph. This man says he needs the trailer more than we do. We're giving it to him."

As I followed her out onto the side of the road, I looked around and saw we had stopped where there was nothing except trees on both sides of a narrow paved road. I supposed it was what humans call a Farmer-to-Market road and a perfect place for a trailer-jacking.

"Over here, Joseph," Sue said, as she guided me into the edge of the woods.

The man, Rusty, I guessed, followed us. "Cactus, you need a whiff of this. This is one sweet smelling jackass. Somebody done perfumed him up big time."

"Okay. I'll be right there with this nice man who is lending us his truck and trailer. I'm thinking we oughtta tie the three together and leave 'em here. By the time they get free, we'll be way down the road. Wha'cha think?"

"Sounds like a plan."

While this was going on, Ray and Cactus came around the rear of the trailer and joined us. Cactus held a pistol in his right hand.

Rusty shifted his position to behind me. "Sniff his head. Ain't he purdy?"

Cactus leaned in to take a sniff.

I launched a kick with both rear legs as I lunged forward toward Cactus. I felt my hooves connect and heard a loud whoof from Rusty. My jaws clamped onto Cactus' gun arm, and I bit. The gun dropped into the weeds as Cactus let out a scream.

I shook my head hard, jerking Cactus first one way then another. His cries continued. While shaking, I caught a look behind me and saw Rusty laying in the weeds, moaning while holding his gut.

"Let him go," Ray yelled. "You'll tear his arm off."

His words jolted me, and I realized the man was crying, begging for mercy. I had been so mad I was beyond myself. I turned him loose, and Cactus took off running, holding his right arm across his chest, supported with his left. When I looked behind me, I saw Rusty on his feet and limping to chase after Cactus. I wheeled to run him down.

"No, Joseph," Sue said. "Let them go. I have their license number and we've got their gun with fingerprints. We'll let the police get them. They won't get far."

There was the roar of an engine and the black truck in front of Ray's pickup spun away.

Ray walked over and scratched behind my ears. "You're really something, aren't you? Thank you. That was the best Christmas present I ever got."

"I second that," Sue said. "Now, let's saddle up and get on to Robert and Sarah's. Ray, pick up that gun. We shouldn't leave it here."

"Yes, dear," Ray said, grinning. He grabbed a small branch and ran it through the trigger guard of the pistol. "Got the usual bag in your purse?"

"Of course," Sue said. She fumbled and came up with a plastic bag. "Drop it in here. We'll turn it over to the police. "I'll call them now. Mark this spot."

While Sue called 9-1-1, Ray put the pistol in Sue's plastic bag. Then he took a pole with a small yellow flag on it out of the trailer and planted it where he'd picked up the gun.

"That oughtta do it," Sue said. "They'll meet us at Robert and Sarah's. We need to roll. Joseph, you're the hero, but you still have to ride in the trailer." She led me in and tied my halter to the hitching ring. "You know, we really should cut in a window so you can see out. I'll talk to Ray about it."

Sounded good to me.

Moments later, we were on the road.

* * *

After another bit down the paved road, we pulled off onto a bumpy lane. You might wonder how I knew it was a lane. Simple. It had every bump, rut, and mud hole that any lane could have. I bounced all over my stall, bracing myself as good as I could. This was in spite of Ray's slowing to where we were barely moving.

Finally, we stopped. I hoped there were no bad guys waiting this time.

Sue opened the door. "Okay, Joseph, we're here. Time to get out and stretch your legs. The others will be here soon. Ray," she called, "grab the saddle and let's get ready for the show."

Saddle? What kind of show was I supposed to be in that included a saddle? Could it be a Christmas rodeo with a burro act I'd have to learn? I didn't like that idea, not at all. My life was herding cattle, not running around some corral making a fool of myself.

Ray joined us, carrying a small western saddle. After throwing a blanket across my back, he placed the saddle on me. Strangely enough, it seemed to fit perfectly.

"Now Joseph," Sue said, "You behave yourself today. Noel is a precious little thing, and I expect you to make us proud."

And make you richer, I thought, since Noel was obviously my next owner.

Ray cinched me up, then led me around the front yard. I won't say the saddle felt natural, but I could live with it. I owed that and more to Sue and Ray.

"Oh, here come the police," Sue said, as a patrol car pulled into the front yard.

Two policemen stepped out. "Afternoon, ma'am. I'm Corporal Jacobs and this is Officer Lemons. We received an alert for this address. Did someone call for us?"

"Yes. I did," Sue said. "My name is Sue. This is my husband, Ray, and this is Joseph, the hero of the hour."

"Okay," Corporal Jacobs said, smiling. "Why do you need us?"

Sue said, "We were headed over here, pulling our horse trailer when we saw a pickup alongside the road. There was a man in the road waving his arms for us to stop. Ray pulled over and— Oh, here they come." Her attention had shifted toward the house. "Let's get ready to have some fun."

I looked to where she indicated and saw three humans coming toward us—a man, a woman, and a small one in a wheelchair.

Corporal Jacobs flipped his notepad closed. "You know you should have stayed at the scene, don't you? Leaving it unguarded could compromise it."

Sue smiled. "Let me introduce everyone."

When they joined us, she said, "Ray, you remember Robert and Sarah from church, don't you? And this beautiful young lady is Noel. Robert, Sarah, Noel, this is my husband, Ray, and these two policemen are Corporal Jacobs and Officer Lemons. They're here to investigate what happened to us on the way over here. Oh, this beautiful burro is Joseph, the hero of the day."

Noel clapped her hands. "Santa, letter," she yelled. "Horsey-ride."

I looked at Sue, wondering what was going on, but all I saw was a big Sue-smile. One of those she uses when the world is perfect for her. I switched to Ray, and he wore an expression not far from how I felt, a bit of apprehension.

Sue said, "The officers were asking me why we didn't stay at the scene of the crime until they arrived. Well, officers," she looked at Noel, "this is why. What choice would you have made? Noel was expecting us."

Jacobs said, "Maybe Ray could finish giving us the details while you entertain your friends."

Robert spoke up. "I think that's a great idea. I'd like to know, too. I'm in the dark."

"Take Joseph with you," Sue said. "I haven't told him his part in today."

With Ray leading, we walked off several yards.

Ray gave the officers a rundown on what happened when the two hoodlums stopped us, maybe overemphasizing my part in it.

Robert said, "That is some story. I am indebted to you forever for putting Noel first." He turned to the officers. "My daughter is four-years-old and has a terminal cancer. The doctors only give her a few more weeks, at best. She wrote Santa and told him what she wanted most for Christmas was a *horsey-ride*. Well, obviously, she's too frail to put up on a horse, so Sarah and I were resigned to her being disappointed. We hated the thought of it not happening, but what could we do? Well, a couple of Sundays ago at church, I mentioned it to a group of the ladies. Sue was there. Afterwards, she took me off to the side and said she might be able to help. She'd let me know. Sure enough, she called and said Noel's wish could come true. I think what we have here today some would call a Christmas miracle. I am so grateful. Our little angel will not be disappointed."

Now, you might think us burros wouldn't understand the context of such a conversation among the humans. Wrong. I understood perfectly. And I vowed to give Noel the best *horsey-ride* any human ever had.

The officers looked at one another, then Jacobs said, "Do you mind if we hang around? This is simply too fabulous to walk away from."

"What about the crime scene," Ray said.

"With the details you gave us, it can wait awhile. You've got the gun, and we'll take your statements later. Besides, I suspect we'll get a call from a doctor about a couple of strange injuries, and we'll have our perps in handcuffs. We'd really like to watch Joseph give Noel her *horsey-ride*."

"Now, that's a plan," Ray said, glancing at Robert. "Unless someone has an objection."

"Love to have you here," Robert said. "First the ride, then refreshments."

We re-joined Sue, Sarah, and Noel.

"Are you ready for your *horsey-ride*?" Robert asked, kneeling in front of Noel's wheelchair.

"Oh yes, oh yes," Noel said, bouncing up and down.

"Then, let's get it done." He lifted her and placed her in the saddle on my back. "Hold on to this." He placed her hands on the saddle horn, then took my reins and led out.

I followed, holding my back as straight as I could and trying not to bounce up and down. Noel squealed and laughed. What can I say? There were six adult humans there, but no one, not a single one was prouder than I. Having Noel on my back gave me feelings I'd never known before.

We made a circuit with Robert, then Sarah took the reins, and we continued around again. This was followed by first Sue and then Ray leading me around the yard. To my surprise, Corporal Jacobs asked if he could take her around. That was followed by Officer Lemons. By the time we finished that circuit, my chest felt like it might burst from the pride and joy I was feeling. Noel sat quietly on my back.

Robert reached to lift her from the saddle.

She cried, "Me. Me. Horsey-ride."

I watched as Robert examined her, then turned to his wife. "Sarah, she wants to ride alone. What do you think?"

"Oh, my. She might fall off."

"Suppose I walk behind Joseph and be ready to jump if she starts to tilt?" He sniffed. "She doesn't have much time left."

"Horsey-ride. Me. Me."

"Okay, okay," Sarah said. "But please be careful, Joseph. Don't let her fall. Please, please."

Robert looped my reins around the saddle horn, put Noel's hands on them, then stepped back. "Okay, Joseph. She's all yours."

I have never felt so important before or since. They were trusting me with their most precious daughter. I vowed it would be a perfect trip around the yard.

And it was. Noel squealed, kicked, laughed, bounced, and seemed to thoroughly enjoy it. I've never been so aware of a situation. If she leaned to the left, I leaned to the right to compensate. If she shifted right, I shifted left. Every hoof was put down as softly as I could. I sensed Robert hanging behind us, but he never had to step up. I walked slower than I've ever walked in my life. This had to be a ride Noel would never forget—I hoped for a long, long time.

When we made it back to the group, Robert lifted Noel from the saddle and placed her in the wheelchair. She sagged, obviously tuckered out.

"This has been a wonderful experience," he said, "but now, we must take a break while Noel rests. There are refreshments at the house. Please join us. Officers, I hope you'll join us, too. You have made the day more special."

He took my reins. "Joseph, you probably don't like eggnog, but we have some sugar cubes and a bag of oats I think you'll like. C'mon, folks. Let's celebrate Christmas."

* * *

The ride home was uneventful. No carjackers and somehow, the road seemed much smoother. When we arrived, everyone rushed over to greet us. I've never felt so loved. As each of them welcomed me home, I knew I was the luckiest burro in Texas. It had to be the best Christmas anyone ever had.

* * *

The next day, December 26, Ray came into the pasture and called me over. I trotted to him, wondering what was up for today. It could never top yesterday, but I was ready to take it on.

He took out a tape measure. "Sue says you need a window and I agree. Stand up straight, and let me get some measurements."

I wasn't sure what he meant, but I stood as he ordered. He measured from the top of my ears to the bottom of my chin, then to the ground. He wrote the numbers on a paper he carried.

He stepped away in front of me and stared. "Two feet wide should do it. Next time we take a road trip, you'll enjoy it a lot more. Be patient. I'm gonna cut you a window."

* * *

Soon, things settled back into their familiar pattern. I watched the herd, trying to keep them out of trouble. Hazel returned to her grumpy self, and Star was my constant pride.

In case you're wondering about Cactus and Rusty, it went as the policemen guessed. They got a call from a trauma center. There were two patients there, one with stove-in ribs and the other with a severe bite on his arm and nasty bone bruises. They described an attack by a monster jackass.

About two weeks later, Salomi and I grazed side by side in a corner of the pasture we didn't often visit. Salomi nudged me. "Here comes Sue, and she doesn't look happy."

I looked and saw what she meant. Sue was walking slowly across the area between the Sugar Shack and the pasture, her head down. She stopped, looked around, then called in a sad voice, "Joseph, come over here."

I complied, trotting toward the fence where Sue now stood. Salomi followed me.

At close range, I saw her eyes were red and her face tear-streaked. She had tissues in her hands, but was in the process of shredding them. I wanted to comfort her, to ask her what was wrong, but, of course, I couldn't. I could only feel her sadness.

She wiped her eyes. "It's over, Joseph. Salomi, I know you don't understand, but Joseph does. Noel died this morning. She has gone on to heaven to wait for her parents. Sarah said every day since Christmas Day, when Noel was awake, she has giggled, laughed, and talked about her *horsey-ride*. Joseph, you gave her something no human could give. I thank you. Sarah thanks you, Robert thanks you, and Ray thanks you. I am so proud of you. And most of all, looking down from heaven, Noel thanks you."

THE END

Author Comment: Moving along, we meet another of my favorites—Ace Edwards, Dallas PI. However, to prove how important elves are to Christmas, you'll see a cameo appearance by Jingle. And, of course, Ace's favorite PI, Kit Levitt—is involved.

SANTA HIJACKING

CHAPTER ONE

My eyes popped open as my ears strained to hear anything out of the ordinary. My nightlight provided just enough light to cast shadows, each of them ominous. As I reached for my Beretta, laying on the nightstand, my eyes locked on the digital clock— 2:56 blinking at me. I relaxed. It was my usual three a.m. wakeup. Usual, because it came as no surprise.

I picked up my phone, expecting it to ring any second. If you wonder why, it's because my friend and nemesis, Jake Adams, called me far too often at three a.m.

Jake is an enigma. We are the same age and grew up in Cisco, Texas. Cisco was small then, so all the kids were friends and played together. Jake and I competed in about every aspect of young life—sports, girls, academics, girls, you name it. Oh, did I mention girls? While it hurts to admit it, he won in each and every one of those.

His father was the richest man in Cisco. My dad owned and operated a drug store. He was starting quarterback on the football team and won a scholarship to college. I rode the bench as a backup running back and paid my way through college. Academically, he was top of our class. I won't mention my marks. And girls, oh my.

In spite of all that, he was like my *big brother*, always there for me. Seemed like one day, we were casual friends, and the next, he was my best bud. If I needed tutoring in a subject, he was there doing it. Trying out for a sports team, he took me aside and drilled. Girls, he set up double dates to include me, always with the loveliest in the area. His protectiveness and assistance continued into our adult years. While he grew richer and moved into the upper crust of Dallas, he never forgot me. And that was the reason my eyes had popped open—he often referred cases to me with a three a.m. phone call. I had to give him high marks for promptness. His calls were always at three on the nose. As an independent PI, his cases were welcome and paid well.

If it seems I was a bit on the grouchy side, let it be known I was a lot more pleasant than my two cats, Sweeper and Striker. They stood on my chest, glaring, warnings in their eyes. For any of you who have never been owned by cats, you must understand that my boys were serious in their attitudes. I knew I'd pay for it later. They had numerous ways to punish me.

I watched the clock. 2:57, 2:58, 2:59, then *The Eyes of Texas* sounded, my special ring.

"What's up, Jake."

"Hope I didn't wake you, Ace. Got a favor I need to ask."

"Wake? Of course not. I always take the boys for a walk at three in the morning. They find it so much more relaxing to be out when witches rule the darkness."

A big laugh came through the phone. "Another reason I love chatting with you. You have such a wonderful sense of humor."

"Jake. It's three o'clock. What's on your mind?"

"Oh, you're ready to talk business. That's fine with me. Got a pen and paper?"

"Spit it out." Yes, I sounded grumpy because I was.

There was silence, then Jake said, "It's a job, an important one—I'd appreciate your taking it on."

"What's up, Jake? You're sounding strange, even for you."

"One of my employees, an accountant, came to me this morning with what he called a dilemma and needed advice. He's a good man, so I encouraged him to speak up. He spun out a yarn that was . . . was . . . Well, it's kinda on the strange side. He asked if I knew anyone who could help him. Naturally, I told him about you. He'll be in touch in the morning."

"So, what's his story?" I asked. "And it would be nice to have a name." Still grumpy.

"His name is John. John Hightower. It's better if he tells you. I . . . I might confuse the facts."

"Jake, you're doing a circle about the May Pole and it's December. What is this case you're butter-fingering about?"

"He'll call you in the morning."

The line went dead.

The cats continued to glare, their eyes achieving the slit and shade of green only felines can summon. Made me glad they weren't lion-sized.

* * *

The next morning, I got up on my schedule, took care of the cats—blessed myself they didn't need a walk—and prepared to face the day. Since Jake had not said when Hightower would call, I followed my normal routine for cold December days—cold cereal and hot coffee. I was in the midst of breakfast when the phone rang.

Both cats came racing into the kitchen from whatever mischief they'd been in as I reached for the phone. They settled on their haunches, staring up at me, their *you'd better share* look on their faces.

"Ace Edwards, here," I said, trying not to look at them.

"Mr. Edwards, my name is Hightower, John Hightower. I work for Mr. Jake Adams, a friend of yours. He recommended I call you about a problem I have. Did he tell you I'd be in touch?"

"Yes. He notified me last night." I wasn't about to tell him about Jake's harassing me at three a.m. "What can I do for you?"

Hightower hesitated. "It's not something I prefer to discuss over the phone. I don't have much privacy here. Can we meet this morning?"

"Sure. How about for lunch at Mario's Pizza Emporium? Do you know it?"

"Yes. I'll meet you there at noon. Uh, I'm wearing a blue blazer and tan slacks. How 'bout you?"

"Just look for a nice beaver grey Stetson on a good-looking guy."

I clicked off and the cats immediately grabbed my attention with their mewling. Then they pranced around before sitting back on their haunches, staring at me, demanding a complete report.

When I finished my in-depth report to them, Sweeper, followed by Striker, dashed from the room. I watched them go, then returned to my coffee.

A moment later they were back. Sweeper was carrying a small furry toy in the shape of a flashlight. Yeah, I know, strange toy for a cat. In my defense, it came as part of a variety pack. He dropped it at my feet, then sat back on his haunches.

"What? You want me to throw it?" I picked it up and tossed it into the dining room.

Sweeper looked at Striker, then both got up and stalked off.

CHAPTER TWO

Hightower turned out to be a short, bald man with thick glasses. He said he worked in the accounting department of Jake's enterprises and it fit. Think of all those cartoons of CPAs laboring over their books, and you have him.

We ordered pizza slices and sodas and found ourselves a table against the wall. Mine was pepperoni and mushrooms. His was pineapple and onion—a strange combination to me. To each his own.

When the slices were delivered, and we'd both had our first bites, I said, "Okay, Mr. Hightower, before we get too deep into this, can you pay my fees? I don't mean to sound mercenary, but I've been burned before." That was true. It was difficult to turn down any case, but more than difficult when I didn't collect.

"Yessir. Didn't Mr. Adams tell you?"

"Tell me what? He only told me you'd be contacting me."

"Oh." Hightower hesitated. "Perhaps I shouldn't say then."

"Say what? Look, I'm not into cutesy games. You want to hire me, explain how you're going to pay my bills. Otherwise, thanks for the pizza." I shifted my chair, preparing to stand.

"No. No, please don't go." He took a deep breath. "Hope this doesn't cost me my job. Mr. Adams said he'll pay whatever you charge. I was to tell you what I heard and help in any way I can. He'll give me whatever time off with pay I need. Sorry, I assumed he told you the same thing."

I chuckled. "That sounds like the Jake Adams I know. He and I go back a long way, but as peers, not boss and employee. He's always up to some stunt." Actually, that wasn't quite right since he'd hired me a few times, but the stunt part was absolutely true. "Now, what's your story?"

"It was last weekend. My wife and I went to our favorite restaurant for dinner. The maître d' knows us and always sits us at the same table. It's in the corner, hidden from the majority of the

98

room—the most private seating in the place. Anyway, when we arrived there was a couple seated at the table closest to ours. They'd apparently been there awhile because it looked like they were almost finished. No problem because our table was mostly hidden by a drape." He grinned. "I like our privacy.

"Anyway, Linda, that's my wife, and I were chatting as we ate when she whispered, 'Did you hear that?'"

"'What?' I said. She shushed me and nodded toward the nearest table where the man and the woman sat.

"I did an empty-hands routine and leaned toward her. 'What did you hear.'"

"'He's going to rob Santa.'"

"'He must be joking. Or maybe you misunderstood.'"

"'I did not misunderstand,' she said. 'You never take me seriously.'"

"Well, to cut the story short, the couple finished their meals and left shortly thereafter. As soon as they were out of earshot, I asked Linda to explain exactly what she heard. The gist of it was the couple were looking forward to getting married, but didn't have the money. The man said he heard a foolproof plan, to hijack Santa's sleigh. His bag would be stuffed with electronic devices, easy to fence. They'd bring in a ton of cash. End of report."

I sat back and stared at him. My pizza had lost its flavor. And soda? No way. I needed a Killian's Red Lager. "Why didn't you report it to the police?"

His face took on a hurt look. "Ace, would you report a theft of Santa's toys to the police? They'd laugh you out of the place—if they didn't put you in an asylum first."

I had to admit he was right. Somehow, I couldn't picture myself explaining it to a desk sergeant.

"So, you told Jake instead?"

"For the next couple of days. I thought about it. It wouldn't leave me alone—and neither would Linda. She kept saying we had to do something. I knew she was right. Then yesterday, Mr. Adams walked through our work area, and I got the idea to talk to him. You know the rest." He stopped talking and stared at me.

I shook my head. "That's quite a story. And, it brings us to today. You expect me to find this man and his friends and stop them. Right?"

"Yessir. Mr. Adams said you're the best."

"Mr. Hightower, there are times when Jake exaggerates. However, as impossible as it seems, I'll take the case. But, it's up to you to help me identify whoever you overheard in the restaurant. Do you have a name?"

"No sir. I've never seen him before that I remember."

I hesitated, trying to find a best way into the situation. "How well do you know the maître 'd?"

"Fair. We aren't best of buddies, but we've had meals together. He's been to my house and I to his. Our wives are the closer friends, though. They've known one another for years."

"Good," I said. "Since I don't know him at all, I can't go busting in asking questions about his patrons. But, you can. So, a couple of things first. Do they take reservations?"

"Yes. It's almost mandatory unless you want to wait a long time for a table—especially on weekends."

"And you were there what night?"

"Saturday."

"Great. Here's what I'd like for you to do. We'll drive to the restaurant, and I'll wait in the car. You go in and talk to your friend. See if he knows the couple who were seated near you, and, if not, ask if he remembers them. Then see if he took a reservation for them. If so, maybe we can get a name, at least a first name. From there, ask him to check his credit card receipts for a full name. Don't ask for the card number, though. We don't want it, and it might make him suspicious, no matter how close the wives are. Wha'da ya think?"

"I'll try," Hightower said.

We finished our pizza and climbed into my car for a trip to the restaurant. Upon arrival, he opened the door and got out.

I put a soft music channel on the radio, reclined the seat, and took out the book I'd been reading, prepared to wait as long as it took.

* * *

Hightower was back in about thirty minutes, which was good. I'd already started the engine once to take the chill off. December in Dallas is not like Buffalo, but still cool enough to need heat.

I fired up and drove down the street to a Kroger Supermarket a couple of blocks away and pulled into their parking lot. "Okay, how'd it go?"

"Great. Antonio helped all he could. The man's name is Benjamin Fernsby—he goes by Benji. He comes in occasionally. The woman with him is his fiancée, and they're struggling to save enough to get married. Which, I suppose, ties into what my wife heard. Antonio isn't sure where Benji works but thinks it's in sales. He's believes it might be a car dealership." Hightower hesitated. "Uh, that's about it. Does it help?"

"Yes, it does," I said. "You did great. Now, what we have to do is track this guy down. And, with a last name like Fernsby, it shouldn't be too difficult. Car dealership, eh? I'll see how many list their salesmen online. Maybe I'll get lucky. If not, there are other ways. Give me a few minutes to think."

I got out and walked around the parking area. The fresh, chilled air helped to clear my mind and help my thinking. Nevertheless, no brilliant ideas invaded my head.

As I reentered the car, I said, "I'll take you to your vehicle. You might as well go back to work. I'll make contact if I need your help again. Most likely that'll be when I have someone for you to eyeball. Also, I'll let Jake know I'll need your assistance from time to time."

"That'd be great. Thank you, Ace. I feel much better now, and I know my wife will be relieved."

* * *

After dropping Hightower at his car, I went home where Sweeper and Striker met me at the front door, demanding a briefing. I gave them a quick rundown on the day, then went to the computer. I googled car dealerships in Dallas, Texas and felt my eyes bug out when there were over four-hundred hits covering Dallas and its environs. No way I wanted to search that many web sites. I sat back, then shrugged, and searched on Benjamin Fernsby, Dallas, Texas. Bingo. Only one hit.

I followed up on his name and discovered he was a salesman for a local Hyundai dealer. He had to be my man. Sometimes, you get the bear and sometimes, the bear gets you. Today was apparently an *I get the bear* day. Next, all I had to do was produce Fernsby where I could question him in privacy. No big deal, right? Yeah, right. All he had to do was deny everything.

I leaned back and considered the situation. I had a guy named Fernsby who was plotting to hijack Santa on Christmas Eve. Apparently, he intended to steal all the electronic do-dads and fence them, then use the money to get married. The married part was, of course, understandable. But robbing Santa was out of the question.

No matter, I couldn't allow it to happen. The first step in stopping it was to learn how and when he intended to do it. Of course, I could pretty much guess when since he probably wasn't going to raid the North Pole, but the how was the major unknown.

First thing to do, get to know Mr. Fernsby. Fortunately, he was in a business where getting to him would be a snap. I found the phone number of his dealership and phoned it.

A spirited voice answered my call. "Cowboy Hyundai, Sally speaking. How can I help you?"

"Yes, Miss Sally. I'm interested in speaking with a salesman. I've heard good things about a Mr. Fernsby. Is he available?"

"I'll page him."

In the background, I heard, "Mr. Fernsby, call on line 3."

I waited a couple of minutes, then she came back on the line. "Sorry, he isn't picking up. He must be with a customer. Can I have him call you?"

I hesitated, not thrilled with giving out my proper ID. "Yes. Tell him to call me at this number. I'm interested in hybrids. Have to be kind to the environment, don't we?"

"Yes, sir. And your name is—"

I hit the disconnect button.

CHAPTER THREE

An hour later, the phone rang. "Hello," I said, careful for once not to give my name.

"My name is Benji Fernsby with Cowboy Hyundai. I received a message someone at this number was interested in speaking with me. Is he there?"

"That was me," I said. "Arthur Edwards. Thank you for returning my call." I went to Arthur for one of the *very* few times in my adult life. I didn't have much fame in the Dallas area, but my successful cases had generated a low-level of notoriety. I didn't want to take a chance on tipping my hand too soon by using Ace. "I'm considering buying a new car, and I'm thinking of getting a hybrid. It's important to do whatever we can to protect the environment." I didn't know whether he was an environmentalist or not, but I knew he wouldn't dare disagree with me. That would be flunking Sales 101.

"Yes, sir, Mr. Edwards. Hyundai has a fine line of hybrids. I'd love to show them to you."

"Oh, that'd be great," I said. "When can you come by. Please bring lots of brochures. I like to study them when TV gets boring."

There was a moment of silence. "Ah, you want me to come to you? Can't you visit the showroom? I can show you actual cars."

"Oh, no. I never go to dealerships. Too many germs floating around. All those people walking in off the street. How about tomorrow afternoon?"

"Well . . . ah . . . yes, I think I can do that. Let me check my schedule. It'll only take a moment."

The line went silent while he ostensibly looked to see if he had an opening for me. I had no doubt there would be a window where he could fit me in.

"We're in luck, Mr. Edwards. How about three tomorrow afternoon? I'll bring information on all our hybrids. I think you'll be impressed. In fact, I'll probably be driving a Sonata Hybrid. I love the car."

"Wonderful. Here's my address." I gave him the street and house number, then hit the disconnect button, a smile on my face.

'Welcome to my web,' said the spider to the fly.

Fine. Step one was in motion. Now, I needed to add reinforcement. Hopefully, I had not jumped the gun. It was time to contact Jingle Bell.

Though I was an ardent admirer, I had no real inroads to contact Santa. And preventing the hijacking of his sleigh would take his full cooperation. However, I did know Jingle Bell, one of his elves. If you're not familiar with my case about helping Jingle on a theft from one of Santa's warehouses, I'll just say he's a strange little creature, standing about two feet tall—every inch filled with ego and trickery. Working with him was an experience as he tended to pop in and out when he felt like it. I never had the feeling I could trust him to be where he should be. Fortunately, upon the successful recovery of the toys stolen from Santa's warehouse, he left me a way to contact him. I hoped it was still viable.

I activated the link.

"Ace Edwards. I am surprised. What kind of trouble are you in this time?"

"Nice to talk to you, too, Jingle. I'm not in trouble, but Santa might be. I need help. I know it's a busy time for you, but can you break away?"

"How serious is it?"

I debated how much to tell him, then said, "Honestly, I'm not sure. But there is a rumor about hijacking Santa's sleigh. It's loud enough that I'm listening."

"That's enough," Jingle said, jumping in. "How soon do you need me?"

"Tomorrow. I have a meeting set at my place at three o'clock. I need you to listen in."

"I'll be there."

He broke the connection.

I sat a moment thinking how best to introduce Jingle to Mr. Fernsby, other than having him swoop in. Only took a few seconds. Shock to loosen Ferbsby's tongue was my preferred method.

I considered what I knew and whether I needed more help. Naturally, Kit Levitt came to mind. She was a freelance PI in Dallas like me, maybe better than me. We shared cases when we had an overload or needed assistance. Once we shared serious emotions and considered consolidating practices and names, but figured out we were too much alike to ever make it work. However, she was my number one go-to person. I hesitated, picturing the hoo-ha she'd have when I told her I was pursuing a case to prevent the hijacking of Santa Claus. No, I'd wait to contact her.

* * *

I spent the next morning researching Hyundai hybrids and getting ready for Fernsby's visit. I wanted to know enough about his cars so he wouldn't smell a rat—until I was ready to offer a cheese tray. Anticipating he'd bring brochures and other sales materials, I cleared the dining room table, then stood back and surveyed the scene. Everything looked fine except . . . except what? Snacks and something to drink. I checked the fridge and was relieved to discover I had enough sodas and the cabinet revealed chips and peanuts. All was set.

All except Jingle. I'd heard nothing from him since we spoke. I hoped he'd show. Being confronted by a Santa elf should produce enough of a shock to spring Fernsby's tongue loose.

At two-thirty, I was engrossed in refreshing myself on the points of the Hyundai Sonata Hybrid, marveling at its rated miles per gallon and all its fancy doodads. I didn't need to be an expert, but knowledgeable enough so Fernsby didn't think I was a total patsy. Of course, I didn't plan to give him very long to make his sales pitch.

I felt another presence in the room, someone looking over my shoulder. When I spun, there was no one. Only one answer. "Okay, Jingle, show yourself. I know you're here."

He materialized, sitting on the edge of the table in front of me. "Hello to you, too, Ace. Glad to see you. Now tell me about hijacking Santa's sleigh."

I filled him in on the little I knew, then said, "The person who talked about it will be here at three. He thinks he's coming to sell a car. I'll let him talk until he's comfortable, then bounce my questions off him. I'm pretty sure he'll deny them. From there, we'll play it by ear, but be ready to pop in if I call you. Does that work for you?"

"Sure. As long as we get what we need to protect Santa."

"Fine. Now, relax however elves do. He'll be here most any time."

* * *

At three sharp, the doorbell rang. I opened the door and said, "Mr. Fernsby?"

"Yes."

"Please, come in. I'm all ready for you. Buying a car is a big decision for me, and I can't tolerate the pressure of the showroom and all those germs. I'm gonna be looking at the hybrids in my price range, but I'm gonna do it on my terms. You're the first, and I appreciate you coming. But, don't get your hopes up. I'm in the preliminaries of investigating the market."

"Yessir, Mr. Edwards. I understand. It's my pleasure to show you why my cars are the best you can get for your money."

I led him into the dining room and indicated he should sit at the table. "Spread out your materials however you need to. I'll get us something to drink and a snack." I retreated to the kitchen where I'd prepositioned peanuts and chips. After delivering them, I poured two sodas and sat at the table. "I'm ready if you are."

Fernsby launched into his spiel, extolling the virtues of the Hyundai line. I listened politely, occasionally interjecting a question.

After about twenty minutes, I held up my hand in a *stop* motion. "I have one more question—the most important one. How do you propose to hijack Santa on Christmas Eve?"

"Yes, the Hyundai Ioniq will— What did you say?"

I repeated my question.

"I . . . I . . . don't know what you're talking about."

I flipped out my PI credential case with badge, then put it away, not giving Fernsby enough time to examine it closely. "You were

106

overheard discussing the hijack. Now, you can either talk to me, or dig yourself into a deeper hole. Which do you prefer?"

"No, not me. I . . . No. I wouldn't . . ."

"Knock it off. Imagine what will happen if I leak this to the media. I can see the headlines now. *Local Salesman Plans to Steal Santa's Toys.* You'll be fired before the ink is dry. There will be no place you can hide. You'll be ostracized every way you turn. No decent person will acknowledge you. Is that the kind of life you want?"

"No, no. Of course not. But, you—"

"Answer my questions then," I said. "It's your only way out. Plus, I assure you your plans will fail."

"I don't understand. Why . . . Give me a moment."

He paused, and I gave him space.

After several minutes, during which Fernsby's face twisted through all kinds of contortions, he said, "I don't know where you got your info, but it's wrong. One day in the showroom, I overheard a couple of guys taking about such a thing, but I'm not involved. I assumed they were joking. Maybe that's what you're talking about."

I stared at him, saying nothing. Silence is sometimes the best ally when questioning a suspect.

He squirmed, looking at everything except me. Finally, he stammered, "Mr. Edwards, you got me wrong. That's the truth. I'm not into anything like that. I would never steal from Santa. My fiancée would desert me in a minute, and she's the most important thing in my life."

I continued to stare at him, beginning to believe he was leveling with me. His bringing his fiancée into the conversation was unexpected. "Suppose I talk to your fiancée about this. What would she tell me?"

"No. Please don't. I . . . I—" He stopped. "Did she tell you? Now I remember. I told her about it over dinner one night. We both got a laugh out of it. She knew I wasn't involved, though. She— Someone must have overheard me telling her. Is that what happened?"

"Sorry. That's not something I choose to tell you. You're making it sound like she's your best witness. Give me her name and phone number, and I'll give her a call."

"I can't. I just can't. She's too precious to involve."

CHAPTER FOUR

I might get labeled a softie, but I believed him. However, I needed to play my hole card to cinch it. "Jingle. Pop in here, please."

He materialized, standing on the end of the table. "You called, sire?"

I grinned, couldn't help myself. Fernsby's face had taken on a look I'd seldom seen before. His eyes were the size of saucers and his mouth was opened in a perfect O. I snapped my fingers in front of him. "I'd like you to meet a collogue of mine. His name is Jingle Bell. He's an elf, specifically a Santa Elf. But that's not all. He's also the Santa-Investigator-in-Charge for the Santa Bureau of Investigation. He and his people are charged with keeping Santa safe and managing the Naughty and Nice lists. He's also blessed with super powers."

I turned to Jingle. "Were you listening to his explanation? What do you think?"

"Same as you," Jingle said. "He's not lying. My truth detector says he's honest."

I sighed. "That doesn't help, though. Someone out there wants to rob Santa, and we still don't know who he or they are." I turned to Fernsby. "Maybe you can save us a lot of shoe leather. Willing to help?"

"Oh, yes. Anything I can do. What is it?"

"First, we'll start with a description of the two men who came into the dealership."

Fernsby appeared to think. "They were . . . ah . . . Sorry, I have no idea. So many people come through. I don't remember what they looked like."

"I understand," I said. "Jingle? Got anything in your magic bag to help?"

He frowned. "Not anything I'm supposed to use on humans without Santa's permission. But, what the Christmas tree, this is an emergency. Mr. Fernsby, do you mind if I hypnotize you? Once you're under the spell, we'll zero in on the two gents you heard talking."

Fernsby looked at me, skepticism in his eyes. "If it'll help, by all means. I'll do anything I can. My fiancée would expect no less."

"Let's get to it," I said.

* * *

Forty-five minutes later, we had a reasonably detailed description of the men. What we didn't have, though, were names. He simply did not know them.

"Anything else, Ace?" Jingle said.

"Give me a moment to roll it around." I studied the descriptions while looking for a solution. Bingo. "Ask him who waited on the two men. Someone must have met them at the door and walked them around the place."

"Will do," Jingle said.

Five-minutes later, we had a salesman's name, and I told Jingle to bring him out of the trance, telling him to remember all that had transpired.

"How'd I do" Fernsby said, shaking his head.

"Fantastic," I said. "Don't you remember?"

He hesitated. "Ah . . . Yes. Yes, I do. I gave you descriptions of the two and . . . and the name of the salesman who served them. Two things I had no idea I knew. You guys are good."

"Jingle is. Now, we need one more thing. See if the salesman remembers their names or kept a record of them. If so, we need them. If not, we'll bring him here and put him in a trance. Will you do it?"

"Of course. I said I'd do anything I can to help."

"Be careful, though. Don't want anyone suspecting we're on to them."

* * *

The next day, I had two names, addresses, emails, and phone numbers in front of me. It turned out the salesman was smooth and the prospective buyers were loquacious about the cars they wanted to buy—after the first of the year. They were happy to give him their personal information.

My culprits were James Johnson and Fred Williams. I felt fortunate I had their addresses. A search would probably turn up several hundred with those names.

Also, like most salesmen, he was talkative and quick to respond to Fernsby's curiosity. During their conversation, he also dropped that he'd overhead them discussing lasers.

Lasers. That lit me up. I knew the eyes could be seriously damaged if hit with a laser. It was not uncommon to read stories about pilots and policemen who reported someone shining lasers at them, and the damage they could cause. I summoned Jingle.

When he popped in, I asked, "What would happen if someone shined lasers at the reindeer and at Santa?"

He hesitated only a second. "Nothing good. At a minimum, it would force Santa to land while he figured out his next step. At worst, the reindeer could be blinded, as could Santa. Is that what they're thinking? No way we can allow this to happen." He was more serious than I'd ever seen him.

"Do you have any experience with something like this, with someone attacking Santa?"

"Not lasers, but yes, I hate to say. Several years ago, while Santa was delivering toys and the reindeer waited on the roof, someone tried to steal the sleigh. He was thwarted when Santa popped up out of the chimney and startled him. He slipped and slid off the roof, landing in a hedge. Santa watched him limp off, then continued on his rounds. Nothing is more important than completing the deliveries. Since then, I've been flying *shotgun* for him—that's what you call it, isn't it, shotgun?"

"Will you be with him this year?"

"Yes. Especially since we know someone is thinking of attacking him. I can't let that happen."

"I agree," I said. "I'm open to ideas on how we stop them."

"We can bring one or both of them in, and I'll get a confession. Maybe scare them out of following through."

I gave it some thought. "No. I don't think that's the answer. They'll still be out there, and we won't know what they're up to."

"Yeah, you're right," Jingle said. "And lasers are too dangerous to take a chance on."

Both of us stopped talking. My mind was toiling as hard as it could.

"Suppose we track them down, get to know them," Jingle said, "then you follow them on Christmas Eve. When they get set up, waiting for Santa, you can let me know where they are. That way, I can pop in and help. In the meantime, I'll make sure Santa and the reindeer have protective eyewear."

After mulling it over, I said, "Sounds good. We'll go with that."

We were both quiet for a while. Then, I had a thought. "What do we do once we stop them? I don't want to leave them loose on the streets. Who knows what scheme they'll come up with next year? Putting them on the Naughty List is not enough. And I sure can't turn them over to the police for plotting to attack Santa. I'd have a padded cell all to myself. And if I offered you up as my witness, they'd double the pads."

"That's true. Humans can be so dumb. Imagine not believing in Santa Claus. I guess we need to tie them to a human crime, something like robbing a bank. The cops would come running."

"You're right. Let's skip the bank robbing though. Something simpler, something having to do with the lasers they'll be carrying. Something like . . . like a pilot filing a complaint they targeted his plane. Yeah, that's it." I felt a grin growing on my face. "And I know just the pilot. Jingle, you take care of Santa and the reindeer, then be ready to pop in if I need you. I'll do the rest. Come Christmas Eve, I'll be glued to those two characters like a mosquito to a bare arm. I'll keep you informed as to what's happening." I knew I wore a grin. Revenge would be sweet.

* * *

That night I set my coffee pot for two-thirty and my alarm for two-forty-five. Both worked to perfection. I bounced out of bed, drawing glares and low decibel growls from Sweeper and Striker, and headed for the kitchen.

Sipping on a fresh cup of coffee, I picked up my phone and watched the seconds tick away. At exactly three a.m., I dialed Jake Adams. The cats rubbed against me, their purr machines on high pitch.

"Hullo, what the hell? Ace, are you nuts calling me at this time of the night?"

"Why, hi, Jake," I said, working to sound wide awake. "Need your help, and I know how much you like doing things in the wee hours."

"You're nuts. Call me in the morning."

"Oh, hold on, Jake. If you hang up, I'll call you back. If you don't answer, I'll come over with my snare drum and serenade you."

"Okay, what is it?"

"Do you still have your plane and your pilot's license?"

"Yes. So?"

"Great. I have a wonderful idea. Don't make any plans for Christmas Eve. Make room on your calendar in the morning, and I'll explain it. Good night. Sweet dreams."

"Don't you—"

I disconnected, grinning. Oh, yeah. Revenge was sweet. Sweeper and Striker showed their agreement by raising their purring to a higher decibel.

One more thing to do, but it could wait until morning.

CHAPTER FIVE

After drinking my habitual two cups of coffee and eating my cereal, I swallowed hard and called Kit Levit. I hoped I was strong enough to take the ribbing she was sure to give. I loved her and she loved me, but that didn't temper the competition between us.

"Ace. What's up? You in trouble again?"

"Sort of. What are you doing Christmas Eve?"

"Staying up to catch Santa munch on my cookies and drink my milk," she said. "What else would I do? You looking for a rendezvous?"

"Kinda. Suppose I told you I had a fascinating and lucrative assignment to share with you? What would you say?"

"I'd say you're in over your head again, and you need me to pull you out. You're in luck, though. I'm sure Santa can find the milk and cookies without me. What's the gig?"

"Not good to spread too much info over the airwaves. I'll come over and explain."

"Okay. But you need to give me an hour to put my face on."

I chuckled. "I love all your faces."

"An hour. No less."

* * *

Once I explained the situation to Kit, and suffered through her jibes and laughter, she agreed to help me however she could. We decided to keep an eye on Williams and Johnson. Odd dated days on Williams for me while Kit took Johnson. On even days, we'd reverse responsibilities to keep either of us from becoming too obvious.

We also plotted our Christmas Eve plan. We'd use two cars, and each follow one of the thugs. We'd stay in constant contact so that if one of us got lost, we could come together behind the one. I had confidence we would not get shaken off the trail.

* * *

Christmas Eve, I was parked down the street from Johnson's place while Kit watched Williams. A car pulled into the driveway. Williams got out, walked to the door, and rang the doorbell. They spoke for a moment, then each showed the other something—a small tube of some kind. I suspected it might be the lasers.

Kit pulled in behind me. "You think they might be carpooling?"

"Could be. If so, we'll leapfrog as we follow them. I'll lead out, then after a few blocks you pass and stay on them, then I'll pass, etc. We'll keep it up until they reach wherever they're heading. Don't want them to know they're being tailed."

"Gotcha, chief."

I might have heard a chuckle in those words. Even so, there was that tone of *there you go again, preaching to the choir.*

Several minutes later, they came out, got in Johnson's white pickup, and headed out. I gave them time to get a respectable lead, then pulled in behind them.

We did our leapfrog thing until they reached an open area between two developments under construction. As they parked in the vacant area, I pulled off, as did Kit. We kept an eye on the truck, but they didn't get out.

I saw two cigarettes glowing in the dark. Apparently, in addition to being thieves, they had a nasty nicotine habit. "Let's work our way closer," I said to Kit. "I want to be close enough to strike when the time is right."

"Right, chief." There was that tone again.

We worked our way to within twenty-five feet or so from their vehicle, figuring their plan was to dump Santa's toy load into the bed of the truck and get out as fast as they could. We'd be ready.

The time ticked by—eleven, midnight, one. I heard a tinkling, like sleigh bells. Scanning the sky, I saw Santa's sleigh working its way toward us. I activated my phone which had been open for the last couple of hours. "You there, Jake?"

"Ten-four."

"Looks like it's time. Home in on me."

"Gotcha."

Johnson and Williams jumped out and ran to an open spot. Each fumbled in his pocket, then held his hand over his head, pointing.

An airplane came into view, heading our way, its lights clearly identifying it. Perfect timing. I worked my way closer to the twosome.

Two red beams shot toward the sleigh.

"Hold it, boys," I screamed, rushing toward them, Kit beside me. My Beretta was in my hand. "Drop those lasers. You're under arrest."

They turned toward me, their beams wavering, then disappearing. Johnson recovered first and pointed his laser at me.

I didn't want to shoot him, so, instead, I did a bull charge, slamming my head into his chest. He let out a scream and the laser went flying. I must have been effective because my head was spinning, and my Stetson was crushed down over my ears.

Williams let his laser go and threw his hands up.

Kit showed up beside me. "Always said you had a hard head. Wonder how many ribs you busted."

Jingle materialized between us. "Strange technique, but effective. Saved me getting in trouble with Santa for harming a human. Thank you."

"No problem, my friend."

"Hi, Kit," Jingle said. "Haven't seen you in a long time. Glad to see you're still protecting Ace."

"Somebody has to," she said. "He keeps digging his hole deeper with every case."

"Give me your hat," Jingle said, "and I'll fix it."

I squeezed it off and handed it to him. He ran his little fingers around on the inside, and I watched it return to its shape before the collision. "That's amazing," I said.

"I wasn't a toy builder all those years without learning a few tricks."

"Time to move," I said. "Kit, bag the lasers while I contact Jake." Again, I opened the line to him. "Have you reported it yet?"

"Yep. The police should be rolling any minute. Make your call."

"Thanks, Jake. Look for my bill, coming soon."

He laughed. "Thanks for jumping in."

I disconnected and dialed 9-1-1. "Hello. My name is Ace Edwards . . ."

A few minutes later, a patrol car pulled in and two officers got out. "Okay, what's going on here? Who called 9-1-1?" His name badge read Tobin.

I noted they were both six-footers and looked so much alike they could have been brothers. Their uniforms were impeccable although weighted down with all kinds of paraphernalia. "I did. My name is Ace Edwards. I was—"

"Let me see your permit to carry," Officer Tobin said.

"Sure. No problem." I produced my credential case, flipped it open, then handed it to him. "Everything is in there."

He looked at the badge and PI license. "Okay, Mr. Edwards, what's happening here?"

"My friend and I were driving by, and we saw these two here in the field, shining lights into the sky."

"I told him they were lasers," Kit injected. "I've seen them before."

"Are you a PI, too?" Tobin said.

"Yes. Want to see my creds?"

"No. I'll take your word for it. So, two PIs are driving along in two separate cars and just happen to see two men playing with lasers. Is that it?"

"In a nutshell, yes," I answered. "Sounds strange when you say it, but that's how it went down."

The second officer, who had stayed near the car, came over. "A call just came through. A pilot reported two lasers being shined at him. He gave this as an approximate location. Wha'da ya think?"

Tobin looked at me, Kit, then turned to Johnson and Williams. "Time to read you your rights."

A few minutes later, the officers loaded the malfeasants in the patrol car and pulled away. They left instructions for Kit and me to come to the station the next day and give statements.

As their taillights disappeared from view, Jingle materialized. "Thanks, Ace, Kit. I'll make sure Santa knows what you did. Now, I'd better catch up with him. He might need me."

"And thanks for your help," I said. "Couldn't have done it without you.
If you need help with Santa, let me know. I've got your back."

* * *

When I got home, I was met at the front door by the cats. Sweeper carried the flashlight in his mouth. He dropped it at my feet, then pranced around like he lived in ancient Egypt where they worshipped cats.

I picked the toy up and stared at it. It was the shape of a flashlight, but . . . No, he couldn't have been trying to tell me lasers were involved. Impossible, right?

* * *

A few days later, I had a bill ready for Jake and was ready to mail it to him. As an afterthought, I added a thousand dollars, then called Jake.

"You'll find an extra thou at the bottom of my bill. The young man who made it all possible, Benjamin Fernsby, is saving to get married. I figured you'd want to contribute to his marriage fund, kind of a late Christmas present and a best wishes for the New Year."

Jake laughed. "You never quit, do you? That's one of the reasons I like you. I'll see that he gets the money—from me, you, and Kit. Like I knew you would, you did a great job. I'll call when I get something else for you."

"Not at—"

He disconnected.

Wouldn't have mattered if I had told him not to call at three a.m. He would anyway, with no regard for my cats—or me.

THE END

Author Comment: Not all of Ace's cases involve Jingle and Santa. Like all PIs, he gets cases that take him into the lower edges of society. That's the life he has chosen.

THE MISSING JACKET

"Can you recover it?"

I looked at the man sitting across from me in Mama Dawson's Diner in North Dallas, then stared at the notes I'd taken in the last half-hour. He'd introduced himself as Aaron Dunniker, Counselor-at-Law.

"Mr. Dunniker, let me see if I have this straight. You want me to recover your leather jacket, which disappeared from your car two days ago. Am I correct?"

"Yes. Not too complicated for you is it? I thought Ace Edwards was a hotshot PI."

I eyed him, wondering if there was an insult in his words. My impulse was to tell him to cram it—you can guess where—then stick him with the bill for the French toast I ate while we talked. I'd heard of him—hotshot plaintiff attorney, not one of my favorite species. But there was something bizarre about his story, and my curiosity quotient had soared as he told it.

That's one of my major shortcomings, an insatiable curiosity coupled with impatience toward assuaging it. Probably what caused me to quit the Dallas Police Force, get a PI license, and hang out a shingle. Not patient enough to allow the liberal court system time to put the bad guys away—when there was a judge inclined to do so. Figured I could speed things up and make a few dimes at the same time.

Nothing wrong with the idea, but the execution proved more difficult than I expected. I still worked out of my bedroom, a fact my two cats, Sweeper and Striker, often resented, especially when the phone rang in the middle of the night. Mr. Dunniker's call didn't meet that criteria, but it was early enough to wake me on a day I had little to do. After arranging a breakfast meeting, I envisioned a return to slumberland. However, if a cat or cats own you, you know what happened next. The boys thought it an excellent time to play and did so. They romped from room to room and managed to hit the bed with each trip. Soon, I gave up and headed to the shower.

Now I sat across from Mr. Dunniker after listening to his tale of woe. I scanned my notes again. "Two days ago, your car was parked in the Dallas Galleria while you shopped for a Christmas present for your wife. Someone broke into the car and stole a leather jacket from the backseat. You want to hire me to get it back." I paused, thinking through what I'd said. "Do I have it all?"

"Can you do it?"

"Well, I can't be sure, but I can try. A few more questions though, if you have the time."

"I can give you another fifteen minutes."

Ignoring his self-importance, I asked, "Was anything other than your coat taken?"

"No. That's all. Of course, that's all there was with any value. I don't normally leave anything where it can be seen."

"Why'd you leave the jacket? Why weren't you wearing it?"

"Didn't need it. It was a nice day, the Galleria is warm, and I parked near the entrance. Never considered putting it on."

I picked up my spoon and stirred my coffee, his story nagging at me. "Mr. Dunniker, how much did the leather cost?"

"Uh, I don't remember exactly. I've had it awhile. Maybe two, three hundred. Why?"

"And you're willing to pay me three hundred a day to recover it?

You know it will take more than one day, maybe several, maybe weeks. Why don't you save your money and buy another one? Did you call the police?"

"The police? Ah . . . I never thought of them. It seemed so inconsequential. I didn't want to bother them."

"Inconsequential? That brings us back to my fees, doesn't it? Why, Mr. Dunniker, why?"

"Uh . . . well . . ."

I waited until his voice sputtered to zero. "Start at the top and try the truth this time. What did you lose with so much value? Maybe something in the pocket?"

He wiped his mouth and looked around as if checking the exits. I thought he might bolt and stick me with the bill, but he settled and cleared his throat. "Mr. Edwards, I must get that jacket back. I can't call the cops, and I can't use my insurance. If my wife finds out—"

"The pocket?" I said.

He took a deep breath. "Okay, but this is strictly between you and me. Do I have your word you won't tell anyone?"

"PI-client privilege. It's our secret unless you release me from the pledge."

He eyed me. "There's no such thing as PI-client privilege in Texas. I'm an attorney, remember? But I suppose I must trust you."

Another pause. Apparently, he made his decision.

"A five-thousand-dollar diamond bracelet," he said. "It was a Christmas present for—" He hesitated and stared at me with a guilty look. "Let's just say it was a gift."

"But not for your wife?"

His head went down, and he mumbled into the table. "Not for my wife."

I spent a couple of moments studying him. I'm not a highly moral person. If I were, I'd choose another profession, but his game wore on my nerves. Obviously, he had a honey and had spent a hunk of change on her. Even a dodo-head like me could figure that out.

"Let's knock off the BS," I said. "I don't work for people who don't level with me. You either tell me the whole truth, or I say thanks for the breakfast and walk. What's it going to be?" I sipped my coffee, then leaned back in the booth, knowing I needed the fee. Christmas was close, and there were presents to buy.

His eyes went through their flitting routine again, then settled on me. "My secretary. She's a very valuable employee. I bought the bracelet for her."

"Uh-huh. I bet she's valuable. How long have you two been sharing more than a professional relationship?"

"What do you mean?" His voice actually achieved a degree of righteousness. "She—"

I slapped the table. "Crap, Dunniker. Would you hire a PI stupid enough to believe your fairytale? I strongly recommend not. You'd waste your money. He'd never find your loot."

His eyes flared, but he didn't argue. Instead, he gave in and told the truth, or as close as I'd get. It was the same stale story. He and his wife had drifted apart. She had her life, and he had his. His life included his young—at least twenty years younger—blond secretary. They'd been *together* for about six months. He loved her, but couldn't afford a divorce because his wife would take everything.

I almost yawned. I've heard variations of that same tale so many times. A few came from the female half of the marriage, but most from husbands.

Once we reached a level of truth, I agreed to take the case. No promises, but I knew a few places to check for the bracelet. When I told him I would ask AMVETS about the jacket, he didn't smile. No sense of humor.

He committed to a maximum of a week and a half. Since it was December 15, that made sense. If I hadn't recovered the bracelet by Christmas Eve, he was out five grand and would need another present for his squeeze. I took his check, written on his office account, for an advance, let him pay for breakfast, then walked into the parking lot with him to examine his car.

It was a current year Mercedes, one of the more expensive models—way more than anything I could afford now or, probably, ever. The usual break-in areas were spotless. The door had not been forced, there were no scratches around the windows, the areas around the locks were showroom-perfect. So how had the alleged burglar gotten in? Not a clue in sight.

"You sure you locked it?" I asked.

"Well, I use the remote. I don't check. I suppose it might not have worked, but it usually does . . . I guess. Do you check your doors?"

I had to admit I don't. "Does anyone else have a key?"

"No." He appeared to think about his response. "There might be one at the house. I remember the dealer gave me two sets."

"So, your wife could have one? How about a maid or butler or even a gardener?" I figured he bilked his clients for enough to have a full house staff.

He scratched his ear. "Any of them, I guess. When I get home, I'll check to see if the extra keys are there."

"Good, because that's my best guess. Either the door was unlocked or someone with a key got in. There are no signs of forced entry."

He gave me a look. "Three hundred a day for that?"

* * *

I watched him drive away wondering if it was worth the effort. I have a low regard for guys who ignore their wedding vows. I've seen too many of them along the way, and the old *my wife doesn't understand me* doesn't cut it anymore. Doesn't matter whether he, or for that matter she, is rich or poor, the bottom line is something fresh struck their sexual fancy.

He'd given me a picture of the bracelet, one his honey gave him, cut from a magazine, and circled in bright red lipstick. Dramatic way to announce what she wanted for Christmas. Five thousand dollars. Yeah, it looked good, a tennis bracelet with lots of diamond chips and yellow gold. No doubt about it, rich guys had an advantage.

Whoever stole it would either use it or sell it. If he chose the former, I'd never find it. There were probably hundreds stolen and never recovered each year. However, if he chose to fence it, I had a chance. So that was my first step as it usually is in the case of thefts. Find the fence who bought it, and work back from there.

Sitting in my car, I called Tom Roberts, my former partner on the Dallas Police Force. He was now a computer guru, having stepped away from police work about the same time I did. But once a cop, always a cop. He kept up with what happened on the street.

After we exchanged small talk consisting of the same insults we always used, I said, "Need you to do some checking for me." I described the bracelet and gave him the stock number. Of course, he laughed when I told him it was in the pocket of a black leather coat.

"Could be worse," he said. "You could have said it was a Hell's Angels jacket." His laughter let me know his opinion of my case. "When do I get paid for my time? It's the Christmas season. You could surprise me with money, you know."

"Not a problem," I said. "You get half of everything Santa leaves me."

"Oh, yeah. Like I need more coal." He laughed some more, promised to find out what he could, then rang off.

I stared at my phone, wanting to call Kit. No point. She was in Austin on a case of her own, a homicide. The wife of the murdered man hired her. I'd trade cases in a nanosecond.

Oh, Kit was Kit Carsen Levitt, a lovely female PI in Dallas. Her given name was Carsen, so that automatically triggered the nickname Kit. What can I say? It's a Western thing.

My cell chirped low battery, so I decided to head for home. Nothing to do except contact some of my snitches and a few fences who sometimes told me the truth. For that, I needed a working phone. Besides, my house phone was more comfortable. I hadn't joined the phone-in-the-ear generation.

At home I was greeted by my two orange alley cats, Sweeper and Striker. Lest you think they were glad to see me, let me put that thought to rest. They were letting me know their food dishes were empty. I'd only given them a three-day supply when I left for my meeting with Dunniker. Someday, I'm going to pull up the carpets and look under the furniture. They must hide it somewhere. No cat can eat that much.

I refilled their dishes, then grabbed my house phone and address book and settled into my recliner. The boys joined me in their usual positions, Striker curled in my lap, and Sweeper in his sphinx position on the arm of the chair. They insisted on a briefing before allowing me to conduct my business.

I gave them a rundown on the case while they listened intently. Striker, who has the higher morals of the two, gave me a stern look, jumped down, and disappeared toward the kitchen. He obviously did not approve of Dunniker's behavior. Sweeper waited a moment as if hoping for more, probably something gory, but when I told him that was it, he followed his brother. Soon I heard the crunching of cat food.

I put out the word to my sources. When I added that a leather jacket was also involved, they laughed, offering to strip search any females they saw wearing one.

* * *

I slept in the next morning, hoping for a late night with clues galore—or that's what I told myself. Actually, it was a lazy, rainy, cold day, and I didn't feel like getting up. The boys cooperated by keeping the noise down to a small cacophony.

When I came out of the shower about nine, the phone was ringing. "Ace Edwards," I said.

"Nice to know I have the right number," Tom said. He then proceeded to needle me for answering with my name.

I was used to it. Kit did the same thing, so I ignored him and said, "And why, my erstwhile friend, are you calling so early? I thought you computer guys worked all night and slept all day."

"I would have except a jangling phone woke me. Remember Joe Napoli?"

"Sure. Chicago guy that moved south. Runs Napoli's Pawnshop. What about him?"

"He called. And it's Napoli's Pawn and Used Jewelry. You might want to talk to him. It's a strange story, one you can appreciate." He chuckled. "Be nice to him. He's a straight shooter."

"Hey, I love everyone. He's my best friend."

"Uh-huh. Just don't quiz him on the origins of anything in the store. Remember, it's legal."

It was my turn to laugh. "Yeah. Guy out of Chicago that runs a used jewelry operation. Of course, he's legit."

"Pretend then," Tom said. "I told him you'd be by late morning."

After a few more insults, we hung up. The cats stared at me.

"Gotta go out," I said. "Hot lead."

They strutted toward the kitchen.

* * *

I parked in front of Napoli's Pawn and Used Jewelry at ten, got out and walked in. "Joe, my dear friend," I said. "Tom says you have something for me."

He eyed me, apparently not returning my gracious feelings.

"You're parked in my loading zone. Wanna move your car?"

"Nice spot," I said. "Really convenient for anyone wanting to hock something in a hurry."

"Those people park in back," he said, smiling. "I have a special entrance with a metal detector."

I laughed. "You're good, Joe, darn good. Tom Roberts said I should chat with you."

"Yeah. He said you'd be by. Enough to make a guy lose his memory."

"Okay, so I gave you a rough time when we first met. What? You carry a grudge?"

"You could move your car." He uttered a sound I took to be a laugh. "It's your lucky day. I'm in a real Christmas mood. Come into my office, and I'll tell you a story."

"Does it have Santa, reindeer, and elves? I love Christmas stories."

The look he gave me said he probably got coal in his stocking.

I followed him and was soon ensconced in a comfortable chair across from a large desk. Joe opened a fridge that blended into the wall and pulled out a Killian's. "Tom says this is your brand. I'd offer you a grappa, but I doubt you could handle it."

"It's a bit early for me," I said, eyeing my watch. "I have a rule. No alcohol until the sun crosses the vertical."

"Your loss," he said. "I'm going to have a small shot. I always talk better when my friends join me in a drink."

It wasn't a hard twist of my arm, but it worked. I took the beer. "Nice window," I said, pointing into the store. "Two-way mirror?"

"You're so suspicious. I trust my customers."

"Uh-huh. Two-way mirror?"

"Of course." He laughed a deep laugh and poured grappa into a shot glass. "*Salute*," he said as he downed his drink.

What could I do? My motto is never insult your host. I chugged half my Killian's. "I saved the second half for you." I held up my bottle. "To your health."

His laugh was bigger. "*Un momento*." He refilled the shot glass, raised it in my direction, then tossed it down.

I finished my beer. "You do this with all your customers?"

"Only my dear friends. Tom says you're one of them. Okay, what are you looking for?"

I showed him the picture of the bracelet. "I have a client who had this lifted from his car at the Galleria. It was in the pocket of a black leather jacket."

He rubbed his chin and squinted at the image. After pulling his earlobe, scratching his jaw, and various other deep-in-thought gestures, he said, "Okay. It might fit, but it might not."

"What?" I said. "Why are you hemming and hawing so?"

"Because I haven't seen this bracelet." He tapped the paper. "But I had a phone call that might apply."

"Tell me. I'm all ears."

"Yeah, they do stand out." Another laugh. "Okay. About a week ago, I received a call from a woman wanting to know the value of a piece of jewelry. When I asked for details, she described a bracelet that fits this one. I told her she'd have to bring it in. She responded by quoting its price, five grand, and said it was brand new. When I told her that didn't change anything, I still had to see it, she hung up." He leaned back in his plush chair, playing with the shot glass. "That's it."

It was my turn to tug an ear lobe. "Do you think she had the bracelet?" If she did, I was out of luck since Dunniker hadn't bought it a week ago.

"I have no way of knowing." He paused. "Look, I get lots of kooky phone calls. Hers may be one of them, but when Tom described the bracelet, the coincidence was a bit much." He tapped the picture again. "This fits."

I thanked Joe and promised I'd return to do my Christmas shopping.

"Don't park in my loading zone."

After abandoning Joe's parking space, I called Dunniker's office.

Three layers of people paid to protect his privacy tried to stall me, but he finally picked up. "You have the bracelet?"

Ignoring his question, I asked my own, "When did your honey give you the picture?"

"Ah . . . I think it was Thanksgiving. Why?"

"I'll get back to you." I hung up.

My mind swirled, but only one possibility rose to the top of the whirlpool. The classic case of young woman, older man. He pays to enjoy, and she collects. Nothing else made any sense. She'd given him the picture, expected he'd come through for her, then shopped around for a best price. I wondered how many other used jewelry dealers had gotten such a call. I'd ask Tom to check it out. He knew several that would answer his queries. But before I did, my curiosity about Dunniker's sweetheart grew. If it were a simple gold digger case, it should be pretty easy to wrap. He wouldn't like it, but . . . That's life. Women have what men want. Men make fools of themselves to get it.

I drove home where I could work more comfortably. After settling into my recliner and briefing the boys, I called Dunniker again. Striker jumped down, but Sweeper waited for every tiny morsel of detail.

"What's your secretary's name?" I said.

"Why do you ask?"

"Look, Mr. D. You hired me to find whoever stole the bracelet from your car. That means I ask the questions, and you answer them." If that sounds rude, I can only say he was a plaintiff attorney. Not a profession on my top ten list.

"What about my jacket? It was my favorite."

"Same rules. Now, what's your honey's name?"

He hesitated, and I could almost hear the wheels turning. Finally, he said, "Cybil."

"Good start. Cybil who? She's your secretary. Surely you know her last name."

"Mr. Edwards. Must I remind you that you work for me? I can't imagine why you're interested in Cybil."

"We've moved on from there," I said. "But, I'll answer. All you gotta say is, you're fired, and I quit asking questions. I'm not too fond of you anyway."

There was silence on the line, and I let it grow. The next move was his. I was irritated enough to not care which way he swung.

"Cybil Rochester."

"Address?"

"Damn, Edwards."

"Address?"

"12356 North Cloverdale Circle. That's in North Dallas."

I wrote it down. "That wasn't so bad was it? Is she at work

today?"

"No, she took a day of vacation. Said she had Christmas shopping to do."

"Okay. What about her phone number?"

After a shorter hesitation, he gave them to me, home and cell, then said, "You're not going to talk to her, are you?"

"Of course not. I'm compiling a telephone book." I hung up.

I wandered into the kitchen, nuked a cup of the morning coffee, then sat at my breakfast table with a pad, pencil, and the phone. Sweeper appeared around the doorframe to the dining room followed by Striker. They stopped, dropped onto their haunches, and stared at me.

"Striker, you might not want to hear this," I said. "It's not up to your standards." He promptly left the room, but Sweeper came to me and began twisting between my ankles, purr control on high. Go figure.

I began to dial Cybil Rochester's home number, then stopped. Caller ID. I put the house phone down and used my cell. I had a block on it. While it rang, I practiced my opening line, but gave it up when her message machine kicked on. At least I verified that Dunniker gave me the right number. I disconnected and called her cell.

When she answered, I said in my best southern drawl, "Miz Rochester. My name is Pierre LeBlanc. I work for the Mammoth Jewelry Company in Bat-on Rouge, Louisiana. We're powerful sorry it happened, but we gonna make it right. I'm authorized to—"

"Who is this? How did you get this number? I don't know—"

"I'm sorry, ma'am. Let me explain. You see, we make the tennis bracelet, model number X379865 with diamonds wrapped all around it in the purdiest gold. Well, the most embarrassing thang happened. Somebody switched them diamonds for cubic zirconias. Them bracelets made it right out into the market without us knowing. Now you can bet some folks been fired, but in the meantime, I'm tracking every one of them trinkets down."

"Why're you calling me? I don't have one."

"Huh?" Oh boy, wrong answer unless she was ducking. "Now, ma'am, our computer shows that Ms. Cybil Rochester got one as a present. Are you saying it's wrong? That's mighty unlikely. Our computers jist don't make mistakes like that. We have the best techies and the best equipment in the business. Why—"

"Mr. LeBlanc? It is LeBlanc, isn't it? I don't have one of your diamond bracelets. I do hope to get one for Christmas, but— I bet that's it. I bet my sweetie-snookums bought one, and that's why your computers— Oh, that's so exciting. Thank you, Mr. LeBlanc, thank you."

Okay, she might not be the thief. But I had to close the loop. Wrapping myself in my drawl again, I said, "Well, Miz Rochester, if you do git one, you jist give me a call. I can swap it and give you a ten percent bonus for your trouble. Or, if you don't want it, I'll pay you retail price plus the ten percent. That'd either be five hundred dollars if you take a real diamond bracelet or fifty-five hundred if you give it back."

"But—"

"Let me finish, ma'am. If you trade it, you'll get a certificate of authenticity from Mammoth Jewelry Company. What do you want to do?"

"I told you, I don't have one . . . yet. But if my honey-pooh gives me one, I'll contact you."

I gave her a bogus phone number, saying it was my office in Baton Rouge. After a few more comments, we hung up, best buddies.

Dry hole. No matter how careful you are, sometimes you hit one. My great-granddad drilled a few of those in the Eastland oil fields during the early nineteen-hundreds, and I did the same with Cybil Rochester. She didn't sound like a gold digger. Sweetie-snookums? Honey-pooh? I'd have sworn no one talked that way. Of course, I had ensured that Dunniker had to come up with a bracelet for Christmas, or there'd be only one woman in his life—his wife.

I looked around and Striker was nowhere in view. Sweeper was busy cleaning a paw, a smirk on his face. "Hey, I had to try," I said to him. He ignored me.

* * *

Over the next few days, I received more reports from pawnshops of phone calls from a woman seeking a quote on a diamond bracelet. From what little info they provided, it could be the same woman—or not. None of them treated it seriously and followed up.

The general response was, bring it in. They'd look at it.

Time flew and my frustration grew. It reached a point where I ducked Dunniker's calls. He sounded so disappointed when I said, "No progress."

Tom tried, but his luck was as bad as mine. A couple of nights, we split beers in commiseration. What had started as a simple chase-the-loot case had turned into the perfect crime.

Even Joe Napoli felt sorry for me. I dropped by his shop a couple of times hoping he'd received another call. Nope. Nothing new from him. But he did remind me each time not to park in his loading zone.

The morning of December 21, I faced the fact I had lost. I had trod every trail I could think of, and none of them led to the bracelet. I called Dunniker and gave him the bad news. He was not thrilled with me.

"Mr. D," I said. "I'm out of leads, and you're out of time. If your *honey-pooh* is important to you, I suggest you find another bracelet before you guys take off on the twenty-third. If you don't, you might get more sting than honey on the trip."

"Thanks, Edwards. You're just the funniest guy I know. You have the rest of today and tomorrow. Don't you have any other leads you can pursue?"

"The only idea I have is that whoever robbed your car kept the jewelry for himself, or gave it to his *sweetie-snookums*. It has not showed up for sale. I still have my hooks out, but it's getting awful late for a fish to bite."

"I wish you'd quit with the metaphors. Plain English is good."

"Okay. Try this. I have no hope of finding the bracelet."

"Simple, direct, and breaking my heart," he said. "This is going to be one expensive Christmas." He hung up before I could tell him I'd send a bill.

Actually, I planned to cut the tab in half. It didn't please me that I failed. Bad for business.

I spent the rest of the twenty-first and the twenty-second casting loops, but they continued to fall empty. The bracelet may as well have been water vapor. It had evaporated. I risked another call to Cybil, impersonating LeBlanc again. She assured me she didn't have it yet, but had high hopes for tomorrow or the next day. She asked if I'd be working the week after Christmas. She wanted to use my exchange program.

I didn't rush out of bed on the morning of the twenty-fourth. It was pretty much a nothing day for me. I'd finished my shopping, and about all I had to do was hang the stockings for Sweeper and Striker. I'd take care of that after the sun went down. The later I waited, the better chance their stockings would still be hanging Christmas morning.

When I looked out the window, my feelings dived. No sun, only gray clouds, and pings on the glass. A norther had moved in overnight. I switched on the TV in time to hear the weather guy promise a day of frozen rain, sleet, or even snow. A white Christmas would make a lot of kids happy, but I didn't look forward to the slipping and sliding on the streets. No one ever said Texans know how to drive in ice and snow.

I fed the boys then futzed around in jeans, a Dallas Cowboys sweatshirt, and my house slippers. I did manage to work a shower into the busy schedule, but refused to shave. I decided to create a new superstition—shaving when it sleets ensures three more days of bad weather.

At two o'clock, my phone rang. "Ace Edwards," I said, expecting to hear Tom's voice. Of course, if it was Kit, that would be better.

"Mr. Edwards. My name is Dorothea Dunniker. I believe you know my husband, Aaron. You've had business together I understand."

"Ah." What to say? When I'm representing one spouse, the last thing I want is to hear from the other. "Yes, Ms. Dunniker, I do know your husband. What can I do for you?" Maybe I should figure out the script before I said something I, or her husband, would regret.

"I know it's late, but I'd like to invite you for cocktails this evening. It'll be casual, just the three of us. Please say you'll come. Is six okay? I'm just dying to meet a real, live Private Investigator. My husband says you're one of his best."

"Ah." Several remarks came to mind, none of them usable. I finally fumbled out, "Is Mr. Dunniker there? Could I speak with him, please?"

"He's not here now. He left yesterday on a business trip to Las

Vegas. Came up suddenly, and he couldn't get out of it. I just got off the phone with him. His plane lands in about an hour, and he'll grab a limo from the airport."

Business trip? Yeah. I bet his loyal secretary accompanied him, sacrificing her last pre-Christmas shopping days. Of course, I didn't say that to Ms. Dunniker.

"I'm not sure," I said. "I promised a friend I'd come over and help with the toys." Yeah, it was a lie, but I hate for people to know I don't have a life.

"Please, Mr. Edwards. We'll only keep you about an hour, then you're free to do whatever you planned. I doubt your friend's children will be in bed that early. And I know Aaron would enjoy seeing you. He speaks *so* highly of you. He must really like you. And," a pause, "I'd really *love* to meet you."

Trapped. Someday, I have to take a backbone course. Mine turns to jelly any time a lady turns on the charm. "Thank you. You honor me with the invitation. I'll be there, but I can't stay long."

* * *

At six o'clock, I rang the chimes on a house big enough to fit a couple or three of mine in. If I lived here, I could move my office out of the bedroom and have a suite of workstations. Heck, I could give each of the cats an office.

An attractive mature woman answered the door dressed in a Christmas cocktail dress. It was red with white fur around the deep V neckline. If there was other trim, I missed it. I took a second look and changed my mind about her appearance. She was drop-dead gorgeous. I couldn't imagine any reason a man would leave this woman's bed.

"Mr. Edwards, do come in." She extended her hand, and I fought the impulse to kiss it. Don't think it was any level of scruples that stopped me. I'd have gladly lavished kisses on it with the hope of working my way up her arm. It was the bracelet she wore on her right wrist. Either it was *the* one or its clone. I shook her hand.

"Aaron is in the study. I know you're a devout Killian's fan so I put a twelve-pack on ice." She smiled and winked. "I do my research."

Before I could slay her with a witticism, she hooked her arm through mine and led me down the hallway. It was like walking

134

with a princess.

"Aaron, look who's here," she said, presenting me as if I were a visiting dignitary.

He knelt in front of the fireplace, probing at what I took to be a Yule log. When he turned, I thought I saw a flicker of panic before a smile creased his face. His courtroom training, I supposed.

He came forward and grasped my hand. "I'm so glad you could come. Dorothea said she invited a surprise guest for cocktails. I should have guessed it was you when I saw the Killian's. I may have to watch her. She's in awe of PIs."

I studied him, trying to figure the scenario. His wife wore the bracelet while he treated me like an emir from an oil-rich country. Plus, I suspected he'd just returned from a night of wild sex with his *secretary*. Weird was the word that came to mind.

Ms. D shoved an ice-cold Killian's into my hand, the bracelet glittering under the overhead lights.

After she sat me in the traditional conversation niche, she took a chair across from me with her husband hovering over her shoulder. The beer was excellent, and the chair was comfortable, so I decided to take the plunge. What could they do, throw me out? I'm no virgin at folks tossing me out of their homes. Part of the job. "That's a nice bracelet you're wearing," I said, pointing toward her wrist. "I'm not sure I've ever seen one like it."

"Oh yes, isn't it lovely? Aaron gave it to me . . . well, I should say he was going to give it to me." She squeezed his hand, which rested on the back of her chair. "Weren't you, dear?"

"Uh . . . of course," he said, staring at me.

Without acknowledging him, she continued, "I'm afraid I ruined his surprise."

I looked at Mr. D. His eyes beseeched me not to rat him out. Returning my attention to his wife, I swallowed a smile and said, "Ruined? What happened?"

"Oh, I'm such a ditz. A couple of weeks ago, I headed out to finish my shopping. I wore jeans and a light top, never considering the weather. My only excuse is our garage is heated. When I parked, I realized I had no coat, not even a sweater. But I noticed Aaron's car nearby. We tend to park in the same area near Macy's." She smiled at her husband and patted his hand. "I looked in the window and saw his leather jacket. Just what I needed. He's bad about locking the doors. I nag him about it all the time. He just hits the button, or so he says, and walks away. Anyway, I grabbed his coat, and went into the Galleria."

She showed a mischievous smile. "Imagine my surprise when I put my hand in the pocket. A wrapped Christmas present." She stood, walked around the chair, and took Aaron's arm. "I know I should have left it alone, but I just couldn't. I've always been one who searches for presents."

"Extraordinary," I said, not having any better way to approach the story.

"That's why I hired you to find the coat," Mr. D interjected. "She forgot to tell me. I thought someone stole it." He grinned a nervous grin. "All this time, I had you looking for something that was in her car. Silly, isn't it?"

"Yeah, silly," I said, ducking my head to hide another smile. "But I've had stranger cases."

"Oh, do tell us," Ms. D gushed. "I bet you have all kinds of adventures."

For the next twenty minutes or so, I embellished stories of some of my cases—adding a suitable amount of gore—while enjoying the looks of admiration on her face. If they divorced over his dalliance with his *secretary*, I'd beat a path to her door—with lots of stories.

At five before seven, I rose, not wanting to outlast my invitation. "Thank you for your hospitality, but I have to leave."

"Of course," Mr. D said, a relieved look on his face. "You must have plans on Christmas Eve. Just give me a moment though." He bent over an end table and wrote something on the back of a business card. "Call me after New Year's. I have some other jobs I'd like to hire you for." He shook my hand, palming the business card. "Looking forward to seeing you again."

Ms. D walked me to the door and gave me a wet kiss on the cheek. Her lips brushed mine as she withdrew. "Thank you for coming, Mr. Edwards. I *love* your stories. Maybe we can continue another time."

Her voice reminded me of Striker's softest purr. Was it a come-on? I hoped so.

Walking to the car, I looked at the card Mr. D slipped me. On the back he'd written, *Thank you for your discretion. Consider your fees doubled. Call me.*

Not a bad Christmas, I thought.

Ms. D had the bracelet, even if she pawned it later.

Mr. D got his ticket punched in Las Vegas, and I kept his secret, if it was a secret.

Cybil Rochester had her night with the boss and probably received a trinket for her jewelry box. I hoped the phone number I gave her didn't belong to anyone. She might not be complimentary when she discovered there was no Pierre LeBlanc.

And me, double fees for solving nothing, plus a promise of more employment. Yep, a mighty fine Christmas for everyone.

I looked toward the mansion where Ms. D leaned against the doorframe, backlighted in a sexy pose, apparently watching me. "Merry Christmas," I called.

She blew me a kiss.

THE END

AUTHOR COMMENT: As this anthology reaches its end, we close with an Ace Edwards Christmas Eve. Hope it leaves you looking forward to Christmas next year. I know Jingle, Joseph, Ace, and I do. Thank you for reading.

ACE'S CHRISTMAS EVE

Christmas Eve, the most promising night of the year. At least that's what I believed when I was a youngster growing up in Cisco, Texas. Now, I am an adult and have put such fantasies behind me. It became just another work opportunity.

I'm usually an upbeat guy, a bit on the cynical side perhaps, but never drowned in melancholy. But that night, I teetered on the brink, about to plunge into depression, and had little fortitude to stop it.

That wasn't my original plan. I had hoped to spend it with Kit Levitt, my closest female friend. Not what you're thinking though. Maybe once, but now she was a co-worker, a fellow PI in Dallas. We shared cases when we had an overflow, like we once shared emotions. However, no matter how much we cared for one another, we realized we were too much like oil and vinegar—great as a salad dressing, but separating as soon as the shaking stopped. That didn't affect our friendship or sharing time together on special occasions though.

Anyway, Kit was out of town, spending Christmas with friends in Abilene. She left that morning and wouldn't be back until the twenty-seventh. If I was lucky, she might find time for me on New Year's Eve. I hoped so. I missed her.

Second choice was Tom Roberts, my ex-partner on the Dallas Police Force. Not to be. His ex-wife caved in to their children's pleas and invited him for a Christmas Eve sleepover—on the couch. Usually, she only allowed a Christmas morning visit. But the farther they moved from the harsh words of the divorce, the better friends they became. So he was out as my companion for the evening also.

I would have crossed the street and knocked on Mr. Harbinger's door, but he let me know a couple of days previously he would spend Christmas Eve with his girlfriend. Mr. H was my septuagenarian neighbor, and his girlfriend was Mrs. O'Toole, a spiffy widow he encountered while helping on one of my cases. During a neighborhood canvas when we sought witnesses, they met and hit it off in a New York minute. I had seen much less of him since then.

Even Jake Adams, my rich buddy and friendly nemesis, whom I'd grown up with, was out of the loop—off doing whatever incredibly rich people do on Christmas Eve. I'd gone through my address book—not a thick document—and it appeared I was the only one alone for the evening.

It promised to be a lonely night, and my feelings were lower than an armadillo's belly. So when the phone rang and a woman identified herself as Mrs. Gretchen Fletcher, I was available to listen. Of course, I set my rates higher than my norm, but she didn't flinch. She simply said, "Get the goods on him. I'll double that." What would you have done? Me too. I had two hungry cats to feed and a flat bank account. Life was the pits, Christmas Eve or not.

In case you're wondering, I'm Arthur Conan Edwards, a PI that works out of his bedroom in North Dallas. I'd love to say I'm in demand and can set my rates accordingly, but that would be a lie. Truth is I scrape by, sometimes feeding Sweeper and Striker—my two orange alley cats—the best, but more often collecting their looks of disdain at the cheap stuff I buy. My friends call me Ace. My cats think my name is Meow. They use it often.

I considered my life to date—forty-two years old, failure at marriage, and no loving family on December twenty-fourth. Not much to launch an ego trip. When I thought of it that way, Mrs. Fletcher might have saved me. I couldn't afford the case of Killian's Red Lager it would have taken to get through the evening, and the cheap stuff left me with a terrible hangover. Instead of crying in my beer, I followed her errant husband, Mr. Adolph Fletcher.

The sun disappeared early as a norther rushed in, blanketing the sky in snow clouds and sending a light sleet our way. So far, it melted as it landed on the warm streets and sidewalks. Not hazardous yet, but enough to make one more careful. Mr. Fletcher was that *one*. His car crept through the streets like he had no place to go, no home to welcome him. I knew why I was alone, but why was he? Were he and his wife so estranged he couldn't stand to be with her even tonight? No punch, no eggnog, no cookies, and no memories of other Christmases to share? I felt sad for him.

Marriages start with such enthusiasm, so much joy, and endless promises to stay together forever. Yet, Fletcher's appeared headed in the same direction mine took—divorce court. I wondered if they had children and if so, the ages. I've seen so many children hurt because adults don't know how to play well in the sandbox. Sometimes I think everyone over twenty-one should be sent back to pre-school to reinforce their social skills, especially the sharing part.

I shook my head, realizing I'd lost my rabbit's Rabbit. His Volkswagen was nowhere in sight. Too much daydreaming. I sped up, gambling that the tires on my convertible would hold the street in the icy slush that was now replacing the melted sleet. Soon, the streets would be slick, and a smarter man than I would get off them. I hoped Mr. Fletcher was such a person. Of course, that meant I had to find him first.

There was an intersection ahead. Perhaps he'd turned, but in which direction, right or left? Since there was no traffic behind me, I stopped and looked both ways. There, a half-block down, he had halted to allow a pedestrian with an umbrella to cross. Lady Luck smiled my way. I wheeled around the corner and picked him up as he pulled away. No more deep philosophical thoughts. I had a job to do.

Fletcher continued driving in a meandering way as if he had no specific place to go. Killing time, thinking about his life, I supposed. Whatever, he should head for his rendezvous soon. His wife said she overheard him on the phone talking about a party filled with surprises. According to her, he looked thrilled. When he hung up, he told her his boss insisted he come by for a couple of drinks to celebrate Santa's imminent visit. Unfortunately for me, she didn't overhear the time the extravaganza got started or an address, so I had to pick him up early. No big deal. I hung the cats' stockings before I left the house—the extent of my necessary preparations. I smiled. The stockings were probably already on the floor, the contents spread around the living room along with the magazines, couch pillows, and other items Sweeper and Striker managed to displace every time I left home.

We drove another thirty minutes, and two worries worked at the edge of my consciousness. The first was gas. The needle on my fuel gauge was dipping toward the empty mark. Also, I began to wonder if he had the wrong address, couldn't find the place, or was lost. His wandering up one street and down another didn't give me great confidence in his navigation ability.

Lady Luck struck again when he pulled into a service station, got out, and began to pump gas. I ducked into one across the street and followed his example. Just in time. The thought of running out of fuel on a sleet-slick street had crossed my mind. Having to call roadside assistance would put another dent in my credit card—one it didn't need, one I couldn't afford.

I brought my hand to my brow as his head turned in my direction. I couldn't tell exactly where he looked because he wore a large Western hat pulled low over his face. I understood since I was doing the same—ducking from the weather. The sleet continued to ping against me.

We stood there until my tank was full. After putting the hose away, I grabbed the squeegee, broke the ice crystals from it, and worked at my windows, all the while keeping an eye out in case he drove off. I was working the side when he finished fueling, got in his car, and pulled away. I jumped into mine and followed.

Fifteen minutes later, he pulled into the parking lot of a small bar, got out, and walked in. I copied him. Once inside the door, I stopped to allow my eyes to adjust to the dim lighting. A bored-looking bartender tended the few customers, mostly scruffy looking characters that probably had no warm hearths to welcome them.

Fletcher stopped at the near end of the bar and took a stool with his back to the door. The bartender was busy pouring beer into a chilled glass for him. Fletcher had his eyes glued to the mug. If he looked up, the mirror in front of him wouldn't give me away because liquor bottles blocked it. Tilting my head down, flipping my collar up, and walking with the gait of one of the homeless that roamed the Dallas streets, I made my way to the far end of the bar. The stool I selected sat under a burned-out bulb. I was in shadow.

"I'm closing at ten," the bartender said. His name tag read Clyde. "It's Christmas Eve."

"Big deal," I said. "Merry Christmas." If he heard the sarcasm in my words, he ignored them, so I continued, "Do you have someone to spend it with?"

"Oh, yeah." He grinned, nodding toward a picture standing on the back bar. "Wife and two great kids. I wouldn't be working now, but the wife of the guy who had this shift had twins this afternoon. Ain't that something? Christmas Eve babies. Makes you feel kinda warm, don't it?"

I rolled my eyes, in no mood for warm feelings. "Give me a Killian's. I'll be out of here long before closing time. Maybe you can get away early."

"Hope so. I got a bike to put together." He pulled a beer from the cooler and set it in front of me. "I'd rather be home, but my woman urged me to work. We can use the money, but more important, she reminded me how nice the owner has been to us. We were homeless, living out of our car a couple of months ago when something told me to ask for a job in this bar. It was a strange feeling, like someone whispered in my ear. I didn't have much hope because I'd been all over town looking for work. But when I talked to the owner, he put me on that very day. And gave me an advance to feed my family. Great guy. Don't see much of him though. Says he's pretty busy this time of the year."

A table cleared, reducing the crowd by three. Clyde walked to where they'd sat and picked up their money and the bottles, then wiped down the table. He set the chairs upside down on it, a sure sign he was anxious to close. After depositing the bottles in a recycling bin, he did the same to the other tables and chairs.

I watched him a moment, then turned back to my beer. Merry Christmas, I thought. Hellava way to spend Christmas Eve. I remembered others—others when life had been happier. It was a big deal in my house when I was growing up. Lots of laughter, good cheer, and hot chocolate. A big Christmas tree that we decorated with what seemed like thousands of items. When I turned two, putting the angel on top became my job. After all the branches were weighed down with creches, men on camels, Santas, elves, candy canes, bulbs, bells, and ornaments of every description, Mom and Dad would stand in front of the tree and say a short prayer of thanks. Then Dad would lift me up and I'd plant the Angel on the top branch, the one that stuck straight up. As I aged, I learned to be more dramatic each year. By the time I graduated from high school, I'd turned it into a huge production. I sighed, bringing myself back to the present. Yep, hell of a way to spend Christmas Eve.

Clyde finished his chores and returned to his place behind the bar. He picked up a highball glass and began to polish it.

After glancing at Fletcher to make sure he had beer remaining, I shrugged off my thoughts of Christmases-past and picked up where Clyde and I left off. "Sounds like you have the right kind of boss. Doesn't look over your shoulder."

"You got it." He chuckled. "Funny looking little guy with white hair and a white beard hanging down onto his chest. Reminds me of pictures of Santa Claus." He paused. "For me, I guess he was."

I did the eye roll again. No wonder the guy had been homeless— hopeless naiveté. He set the glass down he'd polished to a fine fare-thee-well, and studied me a moment. "How 'bout you? You got anybody special to spend Christmas with?"

"Nope. It's just another non-holiday for me." I glanced toward Fletcher. "Nothing special about it."

"Oh, it's special, if you want it to be. How 'bout this? You hang around 'til I button this place up, then come home with me. Kids'll be in bed, but we can have a drink with the old lady. Heck, you might can help me put that danged bicycle together. Be a pleasure to have you."

"That's mighty nice of you," I said, warming to him. No doubt he was trying to spread Christmas cheer. Not for me—not tonight. "Sorry, I have to move on in a little bit. Still got some ground to cover before I sleep. I appreciate it though. Maybe that's what the owner saw when you asked for the job—your compassionate side, I mean."

"I wish I could say that," he said with a contemplative look. "I wasn't like this before. Being around Mr. Close changed me." He grinned. "Made me realize this whole world don't spin around me. It's better to put other folks first."

I thought about what he said. Proved again that formal education wasn't the measurement of how smart a man was.

"Check me out, barkeep," a customer said, interrupting us. "Time to hit the trail."

Clyde picked up the guy's twenty, made change, and laid it on the bar—a ten and two ones.

"Keep it," the patron said. "It's Christmas Eve." He drifted toward me. "Merry Christmas, Ace. Lousy night to be working. Watch yourself on those slick streets." He walked out.

His using my name surprised me. I followed him with my eyes. As he passed under a light, I realized he looked familiar. "Do you know him?" I asked Clyde. "His moniker, I mean."

Clyde looked toward the closing door and scratched at his five-o'clock shadow. "Yeah. He introduced hisself when he came in. Said Andy, or Sandy—no, it was Randy." He shoved the bills into his tip jar. "Nice guy. Claimed to be a writer, but I never heard of him." He grinned. "Course, I don't read much. Couldn't afford it before and too busy now." Clyde grabbed his rag and cleaned where Randy's Killian's bottle had left a ring of moisture.

"Bad weather," I said, risking a glance at my rabbit. "Hope you don't live far away."

"Right upstairs. That's the other thing. The boss insisted we take the apartment as part of the job. Said it made him feel more secure knowing he had someone on the premises. Free rent, too. How often do you find a man like him?"

"In today's world? Not enough," I said. "What's his full name?"

"Samuel Close. That's why it's called the Close't Bar. Get it? Small bar like a closet."

I chuckled and vowed to put the place on my list. Great atmosphere.

"Gotta move on," Fletcher said. "Give me a tab."

Clyde moved away, and I slipped a ten onto the bar, preparatory to following. I kept my head down, studying my beer as Fletcher walked toward the front.

The door shut and Clyde said, "Do you know that man?"

I stood. "Nope. Why do you ask?"

"He just gave you a strange look. Like he had a smirk on his face."

"I'll remember," I said, walking toward the door. "I'm last out. Looks like you can lock up behind me. Thanks for the invite, and . . . Merry Christmas."

"Merry Christmas, my friend. You're welcome in the Close't any time."

I stepped onto the sidewalk, feeling some better, and looked both ways. Fletcher stood beside his car, fumbling at the lock. Since I'd parked in the opposite direction, it was no chore to wait until he drove by. I let a couple of vehicles slide between us, then fell in behind him.

He seemed to be driving with more determination, not wandering, as before. I hoped he remembered his destination. I glanced at my watch when we passed under a street light. Nine-fifteen. His turn onto Lovers Lane made me wonder if it was an omen. If so, we were closer to his party.

He wheeled onto a side street, a residential area filled with single homes. I flicked off my headlights and followed, trying to spot street names, but the darkness and the weather stymied me. For reasons I couldn't identify, the area felt familiar. Something about it tried to squirm from my subconscious without success. I squinted into the darkness watching his taillights.

He pulled to the curb and stopped, so I did the same. The interior light of his car came on as the door opened. He stepped out, stood for a moment, rolling his shoulders and stretching, then walked up a sidewalk to a house. Standing under a dim porch light, he knocked on the door. When it opened, the inside lights backlighted a woman wearing a skirt and blouse. I couldn't see her features, but the little I saw impressed me—curves in all the right places. My Mr. Fletcher apparently had good taste. The porch light flicked off as he stepped inside. A moment later, the inside lights went out.

Darn. I needed pictures. One picture is worth a thousand surveillance reports. If I could catch Fletcher and his girlfriend in a compromising moment, his wife would pay faster. There might even be a bonus. I slid out of my car with my cell phone in hand. The interior lights were one of the first things I fixed when I got the car, so I didn't flash the neighborhood.

Scooting from shadow to shadow, I made my way to the house. A moment later, I camped in a flowerbed under a front window, trying to peek in. Lady Luck had gone AWOL—closed blinds and low lights. I held my breath and listened, but heard nothing. Maybe another room. I worked myself to the next window. Same situation. This was getting old fast. I was in no mood for cold and wet, and that's what I was. The sleet continued to fall with an occasional snowflake mixed in. All I wanted was a couple of quick snaps, then I'd head for home and bed. Mr. Fletcher could enjoy his assignation. It would probably be his last after his wife got my report and pictures.

I was at my fourth window when I heard a sound behind me like a footfall.

"Don't move, buster," a gruff voice said. "People who follow me give me reason not to like them." A hard, circular object gouged into my spine. From experience, it felt like either a finger or a gun barrel. My guess was it wasn't the former—no fingernail.

Since I preferred to think my dad had not raised an idiot, I eschewed any idea of bravery and let my hands creep up over my head. "You have the control, friend. Just be careful with it. The life you save might be mine."

"Funnyman. Walk in front of me toward the front door. You want to see inside, I'll help you. There's a woman in there who doesn't like Peeping Toms. You deserve to meet her before the cops arrive."

Embarrassing, I thought. Caught like a teenager with his hormones raging. What's wrong with me? I knew the answer to that one. Self-pity had been my guiding light all night and now it had led me into trouble. "Are you Mr. Fletcher?" I asked, hoping to stall the inevitable. "Your wife hired me. If you'll allow me to pull my wallet, I'll show you my PI badge. She just wants to know where you're spending Christmas Eve. You'll see that I'm quite harmless."

"Good story, pervert. Move it."

The hard object pushed into my back again.

"Easy," I said, inching forward. "Don't bruise the jacket. A cow paid dearly so I could wear it."

"You're a barrel of laughs." He shoved the middle of my back with his free hand.

I stumbled forward. "Okay, hold it with the rough stuff. I know how to take orders. I've been married." I figured my best hope was he'd relax long enough for me to spin and disarm him. Of course, that carried with it the risk he'd pull the trigger, and I'd be a paraplegic—or dead. Took about a nanosecond to dump that idea. If I were lucky, he'd slip in the icy slush, and his gun would sail into the air as his butt connected with the ground. I'd catch it with a deft move, spin on him, and have him covered before his slacks were wet through. Of course, such a tumble could cause a finger jerk. Another bad thought.

Not having any great ideas of my own, I went with his and walked in front of him. He guided me to the steps, and we started up. It was now or never. I tensed to make my move.

The porch light came on, and the front door opened. An attractive blond stood inside the dark room staring at me. She was in shadow, but looked familiar, like someone I'd known.

She smiled. "Ace Edwards, I presume. I always heard you were a bungler. Don had no problem spotting you. Bring him in, hon."

As I walked into the house, I said, "Do I know you? I've seen you somewhere before."

She threw back her head and laughed. "Not a very imaginative pickup line. I expected better. But picture me as a brunette, and you might remember. Yeah, you know me." She paused, then in a dramatic voice, said, "In fact, you know everyone here."

Suddenly, folks popped up from everywhere—from behind the couch, out of the hallway, from the kitchen. A couple plowed through the front door. Before I could do anything, arms slipped around my neck, and a woman kissed me hard. Even in the bedlam, my spirits soared.

Lights went on and the laughter from the newcomers, Don, and the familiar woman only served to confuse me. I squinted at the kisser. "Kit?" I said when she let me up for air. "What—"

"Hey, old buddy," Tom Roberts said, grabbing my hand in a firm shake. "Can't believe you'd forget my ex-wife." He waved at the blond, and the cobwebs cleared. Samantha, with a new hair color.

A hand slammed into the middle of my back as Mr. Harbinger pushed a Killian's at me. "Can't let the guest of honor go without liquid refreshments." Mrs. O'Toole hung onto his arm like she'd latched onto her own personal Santa Claus. Her grin reminded me of that famous Cheshire cat.

Sweeper and Striker ran into the room and circled between my ankles, purr control cranked to max.

"Hope you don't mind I brought them," Mr. Harbinger said. "Ain't right for them to be alone on Christmas Eve."

And so it went as each of my friends banged me on the back, shook my hand, or hugged me, each with a Season's Greetings or a Merry Christmas.

Even Jake Adams walked in, wearing a topcoat I'd never be able to afford. It was bone dry. Mother Nature would not have the temerity to dampen it. He shoved an envelope into my hand. "Can't stay, but wanted to add my best wishes. Thanks for all your help this past year. Merry Christmas." The next day, I discovered he'd given me nice holiday card and a check big enough to feed my cats for a few weeks.

Saying I was stunned is a major understatement. As the evening wore on, I learned that my Mrs. Gretchen Fletcher was really Samantha, and Mr. Adolph Fletcher was her boyfriend, Don. He had led me all over town waiting for everyone to gather at her house.

The evening passed with laughter and a feeling of camaraderie I'd never expected when it started. My emotions soared with the realization I had such good friends, friends who'd give up their Christmas Eve to party with me.

Of course, Don generated most of the laughter with his anecdotes about the difficulty of keeping me on his tail. The way he told it, he had to stop for people to cross the street, kill time in a bar, fumble with the lock on his vehicle, and a few things I didn't recognize. The biggest ribbing came from his telling and retelling about stopping for gas he didn't need because he figured I did. Per his story, you'd think I had a fifty-gallon tank, and it was bone dry. Okay, so the level was low, but the tank still wasn't as big as he insinuated. As he talked, he played with a short piece of half-inch PVC. Every once in a while, he pointed it at me and said, "Bang."

No one believed me when I said he exaggerated. They only laughed harder.

It had been Kit's idea to put the gathering together. She'd told them it would be a perfect Christmas present for me. I agreed with her.

At eleven-thirty, the party broke up. We said good-byes with handshakes and hugs, and headed out. Each of us wanted to be home, in bed, and asleep before Santa arrived. No one needed a lump of coal in his stocking.

"Ace, okay if I follow you out of here?" Kit asked. "I'm not familiar with this neighborhood. I might get lost in this weather."

* * *

Later, I lay in bed, reviewing my Christmas Eve and caught myself blessing Kit and chuckling at how my friends duped me. And such wonderful friends they were. Every man should be as lucky as I. Guess I wasn't the hotshot PI I thought I was. But if you had to be proven human, that was the way it should be done.

Kit came out of the bathroom wearing a long T-shirt.

Christmas Eve—the most promising night of the year.

THE END